Immensee and Other Stories

Theodor Storm

Translated by Ronald Taylor, Bayard Quincy Morgan
and Frieda M. Voigt

ALMA CLASSICS LTD
London House
243-253 Lower Mortlake Road
Richmond
Surrey TW9 2LL
United Kingdom
www.almaclassics.com

Immensee first published in 1851
This translation first published by John Calder (Publishers) Limited in 1966
Viola Tricolor first published in 1873
This translation first published by John Calder (Publishers) Limited in 1956
Curator Carsten first published in 1877
This translation first published by John Calder (Publishers) Limited in 1956
This edition of *Immensee and Other Stories* first published by Alma Classics Limited (previously Oneworld Classics Limited) in 2009
This new edition first published by Alma Classics Limited in 2015

Translation of *Immensee* © John Calder (Publishers) Limited, 1966
Translation of *Viola Tricolor* © Frederick Ungar Publishing Co. New York, 1956
Translation of *Curator Carsten* © Frederick Ungar Publishing Co. New York, 1956

Front cover image © George Noblet

Printed by CreateSpace

ISBN: 978-1-84749-459-7

All rights reserved. No part of this publication may be reproduced, stored in or introduced into a retrieval system, or transmitted, in any form or by any means (electronic, mechanical, photocopying, recording or otherwise), without the prior written permission of the publisher. This book is sold subject to the condition that it shall not be resold, lent, hired out or otherwise circulated without the express prior consent of the publisher.

Contents

Immensee and Other Stories	1
Chronology	3
Part One: Immensee	5
Introduction to Immensee	7
Immensee	9
Part Two: Viola Tricolor and Curator Carsten	39
Introduction to Viola Tricolor and Curator Carsten	41
Viola Tricolor	43
Curator Carsten	71
Notes	124

Immensee
and Other Stories

Chronology

1817	Born on September 14th in Husum, Schleswig.
1835–36	Completed his school education at the Katharineum in Lübeck.
1837–42	Studied law at the universities of Berlin and Kiel.
1843	Return to Husum as a local government servant.
1846	Marriage to Constanze Esmarch.
1848–50	Schleswig-Holstein War of Liberation against Denmark.
1851	First published work: *Sommergeschichten und Lieder*, a collection of poems and short stories, including *Immensee*.
1852	Forced departure from Husum. In the same year a further collection of his poems was published.
1853–64	Service in the Prussian legal administration, first in Potsdam, later in Heiligenstadt.
1861	Return to Husum as mayor.
1865	Death of his wife Constanze. The following year he married Dorothea Jensen, a childhood friend.
1867	*In St Jürgen* and *Eine Malerarbeit*.
1871	*Draussen im Heidehof* (story).
1873	*Viola Tricolor*.
1877	*Carsten Curator*.
1879	Resignation from legal office and retirement to the Holstein village of Hademarschen.
1880–88	Various stories including *Zur Chronik von Grieshuus* (1883) and *Der Schimmelreiter* (1888).
1888	Death of Storm on July 4th: his body was buried in the family grave at Husum.

Part One

Immensee

Introduction to Immensee

THE STORIES AND THE LYRICAL POETRY of Theodor Storm are as unproblematical as their author's life was uneventful. He was born in 1817 in the little, grey fishing town of Husum, in the province of Schleswig, and ended his working days as governor of that same place. Only twice did he leave his native province for any extended time: as a student, when he had been to Lübeck, Kiel and Berlin, and as a patriot, when he was virtually forced into exile under the Danish occupation of Schleswig and did not return for eleven years. And at all times his life was governed by the values that one would expect to result in, or to be expressive of, such a mode of existence; on the personal plane, a devotion alike to the responsibilities and the joys of family life, and beyond this, an intense pride in the sturdy North German independence of his province, particularly in the face of Danish aggressiveness.

Both in its nature and in its scope his literary work is the proper complement to his life – sincere, honest, uncomplicated, direct. As a lyric poet he modelled his style on Eichendorff, from whom he received the vision of a world admittedly not perfect in its manifest forms – witness his poems of political protest – but assuredly God-given and thus true.

As a narrative writer he stands equally in the Romantic tradition in those stories – among them *Immensee* – that descend from the period of his most unmistakably personal lyric poetry, that is, between 1840 and 1865, but in later life the surface of his stories became harder and his tone of voice more severe.

At their most characteristic, both Storm's lyric and narrative writings are sustained by a mood of reminiscence, of meditation, of "emotion recollected in tranquillity". Their subjects are private and intimate, their justification and their validity personal; he himself characterized the novelettes composed in this spirit as "stories of situation". Their strength lies in their honesty; their besetting danger is sentimentality – a sentimentality inseparable from their genesis in a desire to escape in the imagination from what Storm once called "this agonizing reality". He softens the jagged outlines of this reality by drawing across them a veil of dreams and illusions, so that what he now observes, from an imagined distance in time or place, partakes of the quality of an ideal and loses much of the particularity of a "real", here-and-now situation.

Immensee, written in 1849, belongs in this context – its characters live in the middle-class world of Storm's experience, contain their activities within its approved, conventional limits, yet seem almost too frail, too *weltfremd* to represent life in that world or to deal with its real problems. The old man, sadly reminiscing on an unfulfilled past; the sensitive, romantic youth who collects flowers and writes poetry; the simple, virtuous, rather colourless girl of childhood memory, and her pragmatic, utterly unromantic mother – these are typical creatures of Storm's poetic world. The tone is subdued, the manner unhurried, the outcome of the events unchallenged. The emotional range is narrow – but perhaps it is the concentration forced by this very narrowness that gives Storm his particular place of affection as a minor master in the German literature of the nineteenth century.

– Ronald Taylor

Immensee

Translated by Ronald Taylor

The Old Man

ONE AUTUMN EVENING an elderly, well-dressed man was seen coming slowly down the road. To judge from the dust on his old-fashioned buckled shoes, he was returning from a walk. The joy of his past youth shone in his dark-brown eyes which contrasted strikingly with his snow-white hair, and carrying his gold-topped cane under his arm he looked cheerfully at the surrounding scene and at the town that lay before him in the glow of the evening sunshine. He almost gave the impression of being a stranger, for although many of the passers-by felt drawn to look into his grave eyes, few exchanged greetings with him.

He stopped at last in front of a house with lofty gables, gave a final glance down the road and pushed open the gate that led into the courtyard.

As the bell rang, a green curtain was drawn aside from a small window overlooking the courtyard, and an old woman peered out. The old man motioned her with his cane.

"No lights yet?" he called, in a slightly southern accent.

The housekeeper lowered the curtain again. He crossed the broad courtyard, passed through a parlour, round whose walls stood oak dressers adorned with china vases, and went through the door opposite into a small lobby from which a narrow staircase led to the upper rooms at the back of the house.

Climbing the stairs slowly, he opened a door at the top and entered a spacious room. Here everything was quiet and secluded. One wall was almost entirely taken up by shelves and bookcases, while the other was hung with portraits and landscape paintings. A bulky armchair with a red velvet cushion was drawn up in front of a green-topped table, on which lay a number of open books.

Putting his hat and cane in a corner, he sat down and folded his hands in front of him as though to rest. It gradually became darker. As he sat there, a ray of moonlight shone through the window, lighting up the paintings, and involuntarily he followed its slow passage across the wall. Then it fell on a small portrait in a simple, black frame.

"Elisabeth!" he whispered. And as he uttered the name, he was transported back to his childhood...

The Children

Before long he saw in his mind the figure of a charming young girl come into the room. Her name was Elisabeth, and she must have been about five years old, while he was twice that. Round her neck she wore a red silk scarf that set off her attractive brown eyes.

"Reinhard," she cried, "we've got the day off from school, the whole day! And tomorrow as well!"

Reinhard, who already had his slate under his arm, quickly put it down behind the door, and the two children ran through the house into the garden, then out into the fields. The unexpected holiday was just what they wanted, for here Elisabeth had helped Reinhard build a hut out of turfs, in which they were going to spend the summer evenings; the only thing missing was a seat. The nails, the hammer and the planks were already there, so he went straight to work.

In the meantime Elisabeth walked along by the embankment and collected in her apron the ring-shaped seeds of the wild mallow, which they wanted to use for garlands and necklaces. So by the time that Reinhard, despite driving some of the nails in crooked, had finally finished the seat and emerged into the sunshine again, she had reached the far side of the field.

"Elisabeth! Elisabeth!" he shouted. She ran towards him, her hair flying in the wind.

"Come on, our house is ready!" he cried. "You're hot from running, so let's go and sit on our new seat, and I'll tell you a story."

They went in and sat down. Taking the ring-like seeds out of her apron, she threaded them on to long strings.

"Once upon a time there were three silk-spinners," he began.

"But I know that by heart," interrupted Elisabeth. "You mustn't keep telling me the same one."

So Reinhard had to keep the story of the three silk-spinners to himself, and instead he told the story of the poor man who was cast into the lions' den.

"It was night, and pitch black," he began again, "and the lions were asleep. From time to time, however, they yawned in their sleep and stretched out their red tongues. When they did this, the poor man trembled and thought that the dawn was at hand. Then suddenly there was a blinding flash, and when he looked up, he saw an angel standing before him. The angel beckoned to him, then vanished into the rock."

Elisabeth had been listening attentively.

"An angel?" she said. "Did he have wings?"

"It's only a story," answered Reinhard. "Angels don't really exist."

"What a thing to say!" she exclaimed, looking him straight in the face. But he frowned at her disapprovingly, and in a hesitant voice she asked:

"Then why do people always tell us that they do? Like mother and auntie and the teacher?"

"I don't know," he replied.

"Do lions really exist, then?"

"Lions? What a question! Of course they do! In India the priests yoke them together in front of their carts and drive through the desert with them. When I grow up, I'm going there to see for myself. It's a thousand times better than here – they haven't any winter. And you must come with me. Will you?"

"Yes," she replied. "But my mother must come as well – and yours."

"No, they can't," he rejoined. "They will be too old by then."

"But I can't come by myself."

"When the time comes, you will, because you will be my wife, and the others won't have any say in what you do."

"But my mother would cry."

"We'll be coming back," said Reinhard impatiently. "So tell me straight out; will you come with me? If you won't, I'll go alone. And then I'll never come back."

Poor Elisabeth was almost in tears.

"Don't look at me so fiercely," she stammered. "Of course I'll come."

Joyfully Reinhard clasped her hands and led her out into the field.

"To India! To India!" he chanted, dancing round and round with her and making her red neckerchief fly out. Suddenly he let go her hands and said gravely:

"It's no good. You're not brave enough."

"Elisabeth! Reinhard!" came a voice from the garden.

"Here we are!" cried the children, and skipped back to the house hand in hand.

In the Woods

This was the way the two children lived together. Often he found her too quiet, and often she found him too boisterous, but they would not leave each other's side. They spent almost all their free moments together, playing in the cramped confines of their family homes in winter, and outdoors over hill and dale in summer.

Once when Elisabeth received a scolding from the teacher, Reinhard slammed his slate down angrily on his desk to try and attract the teacher's attention to himself. His action passed unnoticed, but he lost all interest in the geography lessons and composed a long poem instead; in it he portrayed himself as a young eagle, the teacher as a black crow and Elisabeth as a white dove, and the eagle vowed to avenge himself on the crow as soon as his wings were fully grown. Tears filled the young poet's eyes, and he saw himself as the instrument of a higher purpose. When he got home, he managed to find a little notebook bound in parchment, and on the opening pages he entered with great care his first poem.

Shortly afterwards he was moved to another school, where he made friends with boys of his own age, but his relationship to Elisabeth remained unaffected. He began to write down some of her favourite tales from among those which he had told and retold in the past. He often felt an urge to add to the stories some ideas of his own but for some reason he found that he could never bring himself to do so. So he copied them just as he had heard them, and when he had finished, he gave them to Elisabeth, who kept them carefully in one of the drawers in her bureau. It gave him a warm feeling of pleasure to listen in the evenings as she read to her mother some of the tales from his manuscript.

Seven years went by, and Reinhard was about to be sent away to complete his education. Elisabeth could not believe there would be a time when there was no Reinhard, and she was happy when he told her one day that he would go on writing down fairy tales for her as before. He said he would put them in with his letters to his mother, but he wanted her to write and tell him whether she liked them.

As the day of his departure drew near, the number of poems in the little volume grew until it was almost half full. But although the book and most of its poems owed their existence to her, Elisabeth was not admitted into the secret.

It was June. Reinhard was due to leave the next day, and they wanted to have a final celebration together. So it was arranged that there should be a family excursion to the nearby woods.

They drove the hour's journey to the edge of the wood by cart, then took down the hampers and proceeded on foot. First they walked through a cool shady copse of fir trees, where fine needles were strewn everywhere on the ground. Half an hour later they emerged from the darkness of the firs into an open plantation of beech trees where all was green and bright; an occasional ray of sunlight broke through the rich foliage, and above their heads a squirrel leapt from bough to bough.

The group stopped at a spot where the topmost branches of the ancient beeches had intertwined to form a kind of transparent cupola. Elisabeth's mother opened one of the hampers, and an old gentleman assumed charge of the proceedings.

"Gather round, children," he called out, "and listen carefully to what I say. Each of you will be given two dry rolls for lunch. We've forgotten to bring the butter, so if you want something to eat with them, you will have to find it yourselves. There are enough strawberries in the woods for those who know where to look, and those who don't will have to eat dry bread. That's the way things are in life. Do you understand?"

"Yes, yes!" they cried.

"All right," he resumed. "But I've not finished yet. We older folk have roamed about enough in our rime, so we shall stay here under these leafy trees and peel the potatoes and light the fire and prepare the table. At twelve o'clock we shall boil the eggs. In return for this you will give us half your strawberries, so that we can prepare a dessert. Now away with you to the four winds – and don't cheat!"

The children looked at each other roguishly.

"Just a moment!" called the old man again. "If you don't find any strawberries, you needn't bring any back – that goes without saying.

But nor will you get anything from us – so get that into your pretty little heads! Well, that's enough good advice for one day, if you get some strawberries as well, you'll find your way through life all right."

The children thought so too, and set off on their journey in pairs.

"Come on, Elisabeth," said Reinhard. "I know a strawberry bed. You won't have to eat dry bread."

Tying the green ribbons of her straw hat together, she hung it over her arm.

"All right," she said. "I've got a basket for them."

They walked further and further into the wood, past dark, shadowy trees where all was dank and still, the silence broken only by the cry of the hawks, out of sight in the air above them. Then came dense undergrowth, so thick that Reinhard had to go in front to clear a path, breaking down branches and bending creepers aside.

Then he heard Elisabeth calling behind him. He turned round.

"Reinhard," she cried. "Wait!"

At first he could not see her. Then he caught sight of her some distance away, fighting to get through the bushes, her little head bobbing about just above the tall ferns around her. Going back, he led her through the tangled undergrowth to a clearing where blue butterflies fluttered among the wild flowers. Reinhard stroked her damp hair from her flushed face and wanted to put the straw hat on her head. At first she resisted, but then he asked her to let him do so, and she finally consented.

"But where are the strawberries you talked about?" she asked, stopping to recover her breath.

"They used to grow here," he replied, "but the toads have been here before us, or perhaps it was the martens – or the elves."

"The leaves are still here," said Elisabeth, as she looked. "But don't talk about elves. I'm not a bit tired, so let's look further on."

There was a little stream in front of them, beyond which the wood continued, and lifting her up, Reinhard carried her across. After a while they came out of the shady forest into a broad clearing.

"There must be strawberries growing here," said Elisabeth. "There is such a sweet smell."

They looked everywhere in the sunlit glade but found none.

"No, it's only the scent of the heather," said Reinhard at length.

A straggling mass of briars and raspberry bushes surrounded them, and the air was filled with the strong scent of the herbs growing among the short grass.

"How lonely it is here," said Elisabeth. "I wonder where the others are?"

Reinhard had forgotten how to get back.

"Wait a moment," he said. "Which direction is the wind coming from?" And he held up his hand.

But there was no wind.

"Quiet!" whispered Elisabeth. "I think I hear voices. Shout to them!"

Cupping his hands round his mouth, Reinhard cried:

"This way!"

And back came the echo: "This way!"

"They've heard us!" cried Elisabeth, clapping her hands in joy. "No, it was only an echo." Clutching his hand, she stammered: "I'm frightened!"

"There's no reason to be," he answered. "This is a wonderful spot. Sit down on the grass over there, where it's shady. We'll rest a while and then look for the others."

Elisabeth sat down beneath the spreading branches of a beech tree and strained her ears. Reinhard sat on the stump of a tree a few yards away and looked across at her in silence. The sun stood high in the sky, beating down upon them with the full force of noonday. The air was full of tiny, steel-blue insects, their glittering wings humming and buzzing in the heat, and at times the knocking of the woodpeckers or the screech of other forest birds was heard from the heart of the woods.

"Listen," said Elisabeth suddenly. "There's a bell ringing."

"Where?"

"Behind us. Can't you hear it? It must be midday."

"Then the town is behind us. If we go straight on in this direction, we're bound to meet the others."

So they started back, for Elisabeth was tired, and they had given up looking for strawberries. At last they heard the sound of laughter from among the trees. As they approached, they saw a snow-white cloth spread out on the ground to make a table, and on it masses and masses of strawberries. The old gentleman had stuck a serviette in the buttonhole of his waistcoat and was continuing his moralizing discourse to the children, busily slicing up the joint as he talked.

"Ah, here come the stragglers!" cried the others, as they caught sight of Reinhard and Elisabeth through the trees.

"This way!" called the old man. "Open your bags and empty your hats! Let's see what you've found!"

"Only hunger and thirst!" said Reinhard.

"Well, if that's all you've got," returned the old man, offering them the well-filled dish, "you'd better keep it. You remember the agreement: no food for the idle."

However, they eventually succeeded in winning him over, and the meal commenced, while the thrushes sang merrily in the nearby juniper bushes.

So the day passed. But Reinhard *had* found something. And although it had nothing to do with strawberries, it did owe its life to the woods. When he arrived home in the evening, he took out his old parchment book and wrote:

> Here at the foot of the mountain
> No raucous wind will blow;
> The verdant branches bow their heads
> To shield the child below.
>
> She sits upon the scented bank,
> She breathes a fragrance rare;
> And all the while the insects buzz
> And chirrup in the air.
>
> The wood is clothed in silence;
> She sits there so serene,
> While shafts of light caress her hair
> And bathe it in their sheen.
>
> I hear the cuckoo's happy call,
> And tremble at the thought
> That here before me, golden-eyed,
> The Forest Queen holds court.

So she was not only a creature whom he had taken under his protecting wing: she also symbolized for him all the delight and glory of his own rise to manhood.

A Child Stood by the Roadside

Christmas Eve arrived. It was still afternoon when Reinhard sat at the old oak table in the *Ratskeller* with a group of his fellow-students. The wall-lamps had been lit, for down here it was already dark. As yet, however, only a few guests had assembled, and the waiters were leaning casually against the pillars. In one corner of the vaulted room sat a fiddler, and at his side a girl of gypsy-like appearance who was holding a zither. They were resting their instruments on their knees and staring listlessly in front of them.

From the students' table came the pop of a champagne cork.

"Drink up, my Bohemian sweetheart!" cried an aristocratic young dandy, holding out a glass to her.

"I don't want to," answered the girl, without moving.

"Then sing!" he said, throwing a silver coin into her lap.

Slowly she ran her fingers through her black hair, and the fiddler whispered something in her ear. But she tossed her head, rested her chin on her zither and said:

"I'm not going to play for him!"

Jumping up, glass in hand, Reinhard went over to her.

"And what do you want?" she asked defiantly.

"I want to see your eyes."

"What have my eyes got to do with you?"

Looking down at her impishly, Reinhard said:

"They have a deceitful expression in them – I can see."

She leant her cheek against her hand and looked at him suspiciously. Reinhard raised his glass to his lips and said:

"Here's to your wicked, beautiful eyes!"

Laughingly she threw her head back.

"Give me your glass," she said, and slowly finished the champagne, keeping her black eyes fixed on him.

Then she struck a chord on her zither and sang in a low voice throbbing with emotion:

"Today I am happy,
Today I am gay;
Tomorrow my laughter
Will vanish away.

Just for the moment
I call you my own;
But at my death
I shall suffer alone."

As the fiddler quickly struck up his ritornello, a newcomer joined the group.

"I called for you, Reinhard," he said, "but you had already left. Santa Claus had paid you a visit, though."

"Santa Claus!" laughed Reinhard. "He doesn't come to me any more!"

"That's where you're wrong! Your room was full of the smell of spice cake and pine needles."

Putting down his glass, Reinhard reached for his cap.

"Where are you going?" asked the girl.

"I'll be back in a while."

She frowned. "Stay with me!" she whispered, looking at him affectionately.

"I cannot," he faltered.

She pushed him away with her foot and sneered:

"Go, then! You're no use – just like the rest of them!"

She turned her back on him, and he slowly climbed the stairs and left.

Outside it was getting dark, and he felt the cold winter air against his glowing cheeks. Here and there the lit candles on a Christmas tree shone through the windows, and from time to time he heard the sound of penny whistles and tin trumpets and the ring of happy voices inside. Groups of beggar children shuffled from house to house or climbed up onto the balustrade to catch a glimpse of the forbidden joys within. Sometimes a door was suddenly opened, and harsh voices drove the beggars away from the brightly lit house and out on to the dark alley, while from the porch of a house nearby came the strains of an old carol sung by a party of boys and girls.

But Reinhard did not hear them. He hurried from one street to the next until he reached his house. By this time it was almost completely dark. He stumbled up the stairs and into his room. He was greeted by a sweet scent which reminded him of Christmas with his mother.

Trembling, he lit the lamp. An enormous parcel lay on the table, and when he opened it, the familiar little brown cakes fell out. Some of them were decorated with his initials in coloured sugar dots – no one but Elisabeth could have done that. Then he found a smaller parcel with fine, embroidered shirts, kerchiefs and frills, and finally two letters – one from his mother, the other from Elisabeth. Opening the latter, he read:

The pretty sugar initials will tell you who helped to bake the cakes, and the same person embroidered the frills. Our Christmas Eve will be very quiet. Mother always puts her spinning wheel away at half-past nine, and this winter it has been very lonely without you. Last Sunday the linnet you gave me died; I cried for a long while, for I always looked after it so well. It used to sing in the afternoons when the sun shone into its cage, and mother used to hang a cloth over it to keep it quiet when it was in full cry.

So now the room is even quieter, though your old friend Erich visits us from time to time. You once said that he looked like the brown overcoat he always wears, and I cannot help thinking of that every time he enters the room – it is really too funny. But please do not say anything to mother, because it might annoy her.

Guess what I am going to give your mother for Christmas! You can't? I'm giving her myself! Erich is drawing a portrait of me in charcoal; I have already sat for him on three occasions – a whole hour each time. I found it very embarrassing to let a stranger get to know my features so closely, and I did not want to do it, but my mother persuaded me to: she said it would give dear Frau Werner such great pleasure.

Reinhard, you have not kept your promise: you have not sent me any fairy tales. I often complained to your mother, but she always says that you have more important things to think about now – but I think there is another reason.

Then Reinhard read the letter from his mother. When he had finished them both, he folded them up and put them away. An uncontrollable feeling of homesickness came over him, and he walked up and down in his room, murmuring:

"The stranger's path was lonely;
His steps had led astray;
A child stood by the roadside
And motioned him the way."

He went to his desk, took out some money and went down into the street again. Things had become quieter: the candles on the Christmas trees had gone out and the children's procession had left. As the wind swept through the deserted streets, he saw family groups sitting in their houses, old and young together. The second part of the Christmas Eve celebrations had begun.

As Reinhard approached the *Ratskeller*, the sound of the violin and the zither girl's song floated up to him. Then the bell tinkled, a dark figure pushed open the door and stumbled up the broad, dimly lit steps to the pavement. Reinhard moved into the shadows and walked quickly past. A short distance further he came to a brightly lit jeweller's shop; going in, he pawned a little crucifix made of red coral and then went back the same way that he had come.

Near his house he saw a little girl in tattered clothes trying vainly to open the door.

"Shall I help you?" he asked.

The child let go the heavy handle but said nothing. Reinhard opened the door.

"No, don't go in," he said, "they might send you away again. Come with me instead, and I'll give you some Christmas titbits."

Closing the door again, he took her by the hand, and she walked with him silently to his house.

He had left the light burning when he went out.

"Here are some cakes for you," he said, tipping half of his precious store into her apron, except for those with the sugar-covered letters.

"Now go home and share them with your mother," he said.

The child looked shyly up at him as though unaccustomed to such generosity and not knowing what to answer. He opened the door and raised the candle to show her the way. Clasping her treasure, she skipped down the steps and out of the house like a deer.

Reinhard stoked up his stove and put the dusty inkwell on the desk. Then he sat down and began to write, and the whole night he wrote letters to his mother and to Elisabeth. The remainder of the cakes lay untouched beside him; he had, however, buttoned on the frills that Elisabeth had sent him, and they made a strange contrast to his white robe. He was still sitting there when the winter sun rose, casting its rays on to the frozen window panes and revealing in the mirror on the opposite wall a grim, pale face.

Home

After Easter had passed Reinhard went home, and the morning after his arrival he went to see Elisabeth.

"How you've grown!" he exclaimed, as the slim, attractive young girl came towards him with a smile.

She blushed, but said nothing and tried gently to withdraw her hand, which he was still holding in welcome. He looked at her, puzzled: she had never acted like this before, and he felt as though something had come between them.

And although he came to see her every day, the feeling persisted. There were sometimes embarrassing silences as they sat together, despite his anxious efforts to cover them up. So in order to have some definite plan of activity during his holiday, he began to teach her botany, a subject that he had studied off and on during the early months of his university career. Elisabeth, who was accustomed to following his lead and was, in addition, possessed of a lively intelligence, participated eagerly in the work. Several times a week they made excursions into the nearby heathlands and fields, returning home at noontime with their collecting box full of plants and blossoms. When Reinhard came back to her house again a few hours later, they shared the treasures between them.

On one such occasion Reinhard arrived to find her standing by the window, draping wisps of chickweed over a gilt birdcage which he had not seen there before. In the cage sat a canary, fluttering its wings and screeching as it pecked at Elisabeth's fingers. It was here that Reinhard's linnet used to be.

"Did my poor little linnet turn into a goldfinch when he died?" he asked jokingly.

"Linnets do not turn into goldfinches," answered Elisabeth's mother stiffly, as she sat at her spinning wheel. "Elisabeth's friend Erich sent her the bird today from his estate."

"Which estate?"

"Don't you know?"

"Know what?"

"That Erich took over his father's other estate on Immensee a month ago?"

"But you did not tell me a word about it."

"Nor did you ask a thing about him. He has developed into a most kind and considerate young man."

She went out of the room to attend to the coffee. Meanwhile Elisabeth had turned away and was arranging the little bower of chickweed over the cage.

"I shan't be a moment," she said. "I've almost finished."

Contrary to his custom, Reinhard did not reply, and she looked round. There was a sad expression in his eyes such as she had never seen before.

"What is the matter, Reinhard?" she asked, coming over to him.

"The matter?"

He stared into her eyes as though in a daze.

"You look so sad."

"It's the canary," he said. "I cannot bear to see it here."

She looked at him in astonishment.

"How strange you are!" she murmured.

He took her hands and held them gently in his own. A moment later her mother came back into the room.

After coffee Elisabeth's mother returned to her spinning wheel, while Elisabeth and Reinhard went into the next room to arrange their plants. They counted the stamens, carefully spread out the leaves and the petals, and placed two of each kind between the pages of a thick book to press them. The sun was shining in the stillness of the afternoon; the only sound was the whirr of the spinning wheel in the adjoining room, or Reinhard's subdued tones as he enumerated the classes and species of the plants and corrected Elisabeth's hesitant pronunciation of their Latin names.

"I cannot find the lily of the valley we brought home the other day," she said, after they had arranged the whole collection.

Reinhard pulled a small white book, bound in parchment, out of his pocket.

"Here is one for you," he said, taking a half-dried flower from between the pages.

Elisabeth recognized his writing in the book.

"Have you been composing fairy stories again?" she asked.

"Not fairy stories," he replied, handing her the book.

It was full of poems, most of them not more than one page long. Elisabeth looked through them, apparently reading only the titles: 'The Time She Was Scolded by the Teacher'; 'The Time They Lost Their Way in the Forest'; 'The Easter Tale'; 'The First Time She Wrote to Me' – almost all of them were in this vein.

Reinhard watched her attentively and observed that, as she turned the pages, a delicate flush came to her fair cheeks and spread over her face. He tried to look into her eyes but she would not raise her head. Finally she put the book down without saying a word.

"Don't give it back to me just like that!" he said.

She took a brown sprig from the collecting-box.

"I've put your favourite leaf inside it," she said, and handed the book back to him.

The vacation was over and the day of Reinhard's departure had arrived. At her request Elisabeth was allowed to accompany him to the stagecoach, which left from a few streets away. As they went out of the house, Reinhard offered the slender young girl his arm, and the two walked silently side by side. The nearer they came to the coach-stop, the more urgently did Reinhard feel that there was something he had to tell her before he went away for such a long time, something on which the whole value and enjoyment of his future life depended. Yet he could not find the words that would relieve his mind of its burden, and in his despondency he began to walk more and more slowly.

"You will be late," she said. "The clock on the Marienkirche has already struck ten."

But this did not make him walk any faster. At last he stammered:

"Elisabeth, we shall not see each other for two years. Will you be as fond of me when I come back as you are now?"

She nodded her head and looked kindly at him. There was a pause. Then she said:

"I defended you, too."

"Defended me? Against whom?"

"My mother. We talked about you for a long time yesterday evening after you had left. She said you were not as affectionate as you used to be."

Reinhard was silent for a moment. Then taking her hand and gazing earnestly into her childlike eyes, he said:

"I am as affectionate as I always was. You do believe that, Elisabeth, don't you?"

"Yes," she replied.

He let go her hand, and they walked rapidly down the last street. The closer the moment of departure came, the happier his expression grew, and she could scarcely keep up with him.

"What is the matter, Reinhard?" she asked.

"I have a wonderful secret," he said, looking at her in radiant happiness. "I'll tell you what it is in two years' time, when I come back."

They had reached the coach, which was still waiting there. Taking her hand for the last time, he said:

"Goodbye, Elisabeth! Don't forget what I told you!"

She shook her head.

"Goodbye," she echoed.

He got into the coach and the horses galloped away. As it went round the corner, he caught a final glimpse of her walking slowly back along the road.

A Letter

Almost two years had passed. Reinhard was sitting at his desk between piles of books and papers, waiting for a friend who used to come and study with him. He heard footsteps ascending the stairs.

"Come in!" he called out.

It was his landlady.

"A letter for you, Herr Werner," she said. She handed it to him and went out.

Since his last visit home Reinhard had neither written to Elisabeth nor received any letters from her. And this was not from her either, but from his mother. He opened it and began to read. Then he came to this passage:

"When one is at your age, my son, each year seems to take on a different appearance. Youth is always looking for new fields to conquer. Here at home certain things have happened which, if I understand your mood aright, may at first bring you grief. Yesterday Elisabeth finally consented to marry Erich, who had twice asked for her hand in the past three months. Although on these occasions she had not been able to bring herself to accept him, this time she has finally made her decision – young though she is. The wedding is to take place shortly, and they will then leave here, together with her mother."

Immensee

The years went by. One warm spring afternoon a sturdy young man with sun-tanned features was striding along a shady woodland track that led down the hillside. His grey eyes gazed searchingly into the distance, as though he expected the path to change its course at some point, but it never did.

A horse and cart came into view, moving slowly up the slope.

"Good-day, friend!" the man called out to the farmer who was walking at the side of the cart, "Is this the way to Immensee?"

"Straight on," answered the farmer, touching his cap.

"Is it far?"

"You're almost there. Before you've smoked half a pipeful of tobacco, you'll see the lake. The house is close by."

The farmer trudged onwards, while the young man quickened his pace as he passed beneath the trees.

A quarter of an hour later the woods on his left came abruptly to an end, and the track led past a steep slope from the bottom of which oak trees a hundred years old and more stretched upwards, almost reaching the path with their topmost branches. A sunlit landscape stretched into the distance beyond the trees, and in the depths below nestled the lake, its tranquil, deep-blue waters almost completely surrounded with bright-green woodlands, which parted at a single point to allow a glimpse of the hazy blue mountains that dominated the horizon. On the other side, amid the green foliage of the forest, stood fruit trees in full bloom, their white blossom gleaming like a carpet of snow, and from their midst emerged the white house with its red tiled roof.

A stork flew up from the chimney and circled slowly above the lake.

"Immensee!" cried the traveller.

He felt as though he had already reached his journey's end. He stood still for a moment, looking out across the trees below him towards the other side of the lake, where the gentle ripples caught the reflection of the house. Then he walked quickly on.

The path led steeply down the mountainside. He was now in the shade of the trees again, but the lake was hidden to open view and its shining waters were only visible for seconds between the swaying branches. After a while the track began to climb again, and the trees on both sides stopped; in their place grew thick vines, behind which stood an orchard of fruit trees, where the bees buzzed happily from blossom to blossom.

A distinguished-looking man in a brown cloak came towards the traveller. As he reached him, he swung his cap in the air and cried joyously:

"Welcome, Brother Reinhard! Welcome to Immensee!"

"God's blessing on you, Erich – and my thanks for your welcome!"

The two men shook each other warmly by the hand.

"Is it really you?" exclaimed Erich, looking closely at his friend's grave features.

"Of course it is! And it's really you, too – though you seem to look happier than you ever did before."

A smile of pleasure crossed Erich's face, making his homely features look even more cheerful.

"Well," he said, shaking Reinhard's hand again, "Fortune has smiled on me since then, as you know."

He rubbed his hands in delight and cried: "What a surprise! You are the last person she expects to see!"

"A surprise for whom?" asked Reinhard.

"For Elisabeth!"

"But did you not tell her I was coming?"

"Not a word. She has no idea, nor has her mother. I kept it to myself so that they would be all the more delighted. I always had secret plans for this."

As they came nearer the house, Reinhard lapsed into silence. A constricting hand seemed to stifle his breath.

On the left side of the path the vines now gave way to an extensive kitchen garden which stretched down almost to the lakeside. The stork was now strutting solemnly to and fro between the vegetable beds.

"Off with you!" shouted Erich, clapping his hands. "Just look at that lanky Egyptian eating my pea shoots!"

The bird slowly raised its neck and then flew off to the end of the garden, perching on the roof of a new building against whose walls peach and apricot trees were growing in a criss-cross pattern.

"That's the distillery," said Erich. "I only put it up two years ago. My grandfather built the living quarters, and my late father had the farm buildings renovated. So, step by step, new things get done."

They came to a broad courtyard enclosed by the farm buildings at the sides and the family mansion at the rear. Built on to the two wings of the mansion was a high wall behind which could be seen the dark outline of yew hedges, while occasional lilac bushes cast their blossoms over the courtyard itself. Sun-tanned men, their faces bathed in perspiration, bade the two friends good-day as they walked past and Erich called out to them to enquire about the day's work or to give them fresh instructions.

They reached the mansion and entered a cool, lofty hallway, from the end of which a dark corridor branched off to the left. Erich opened a door, and they passed into a spacious drawing room which led into the garden. The sun shone through the thick foliage that hung down in front of the windows, bathing the walls in a green glow, while the centre of the room was illuminated by the full glory of the spring sunlight as it poured through the tall French windows, which stood wide open. Beyond the windows was a view of the garden with its round flower-beds and its tall hedgerows. A broad, straight path ran right through the centre of the garden, and by looking down it, one could see the lake and the forest beyond. A wave of perfume greeted the friends as they entered.

On the terrace sat a girl-like figure, dressed in white. As the two men entered the room, she rose from her seat and walked towards them. Suddenly she stopped as though rooted to the spot, and stared at the stranger. Smilingly he stretched out his hands towards her.

"Reinhard!" she cried. "Reinhard! Can it really be you? It is years since we last saw each other!"

"Years!" he repeated. His voice faltered and he could not go on. The sound of her voice pierced his heart, and when he raised his eyes, he saw her standing before him, the same slim, delicate creature to whom he had said goodbye years ago in his home town.

Beaming with pleasure, Erich watched from the door.

"Well, Elisabeth," he said, "this was the last person you expected to see, was it not?"

She looked at him with the affection of a sister.

"How kind you are, Erich!" she said.

He took her delicate hand in his and caressed it.

"And now that he is here," he continued, "we shall not let him go in a hurry. He has been roaming the world long enough, and we are going to make him feel at home again. Look what a foreign and distinguished appearance he has acquired!"

Elisabeth glanced shyly at Reinhard.

"He only looks like that because we have not seen him for so long," she said.

At that moment her mother entered, carrying a basket on her arm. Catching sight of Reinhard, she exclaimed:

"Well, well! Herr Werner! An unexpected but ever welcome guest!"

And then the conversation began to flow back and forth. The women sat down at their needlework, and while Reinhard partook of the refreshments that had been prepared for him, Erich lit his massive meerschaum and puffed away as he sat talking at Reinhard's side.

The next day Reinhard was made to accompany Erich on a tour of inspection of the fields, the vineyards, the hop gardens and the distillery. Everything was in perfect repair; the workers, both those in the fields and those in the distillery, looked healthy and contented.

At noon the family met in the drawing room and spent as much of the remainder of the day together as their free time allowed. The hours before the evening meal, like those at the very beginning of the day, Reinhard spent working in his room. For years he had been collecting folk songs and rhymes, wherever he could find them; he was now engaged in arranging his collection, and hoped to add some items to it from the neighbourhood.

Elisabeth was at all times kind and gentle. She accepted Erich's attentions with almost humble gratitude, and Reinhard could not resist the thought that the vivacious friend of his childhood had seemed likely to grow into a less sedate person than the woman he now saw before him.

Since his second day in Erich's house Reinhard had made it a habit to take an evening stroll by the lake shore. The path led close by the garden, and at the end of it, on a raised promontory and overhung with tall birches, stood a bench. Elisabeth's mother had christened it the "evening bench", because it faced the setting sun, and because it was in the evening that the family usually sat there.

One evening Reinhard was returning from his walk along this path when it began to rain. He tried to shelter beneath a linden tree which stood at the water's edge, but soon the heavy raindrops started to come through the leaves. He was already soaked to the skin, so he resigned himself to the situation and resumed his homeward trek.

The rain became heavier, and it was almost dark. As he came near to the "evening bench", he imagined that he saw a woman dressed in white standing motionless beneath the glistening birch trees, facing in his direction as though expecting someone to pass. Her features seemed like those of Elisabeth. He hastened his steps, but as he made to approach her and accompany her back to the house, she turned slowly away and vanished along the dark paths at the side.

He was baffled, and almost felt a surge of resentment against Elisabeth, but he could not be certain that it had really been she whom he had seen. Yet he was reluctant to ask her, and when he got back to the house, he did not go into the drawing room for fear she might come in through the French windows.

My Mother Wished it So

A few evenings later the family were sitting together in the drawing room as usual. The windows were open and the sun had already sunk behind the trees on the far side of the lake.

They asked Reinhard to let them hear some of the folk songs which a friend living in the country had sent him that afternoon. He went up to his room and returned with a sheaf of papers covered with fine handwriting.

They sat down at the table, Reinhard next to Elisabeth.

"We must hope for the best," he said. "I have not yet looked through them myself."

Elisabeth unrolled the manuscript.

"There is music as well," she said. "You must sing it to us, Reinhard."

He read out a few Tyrolese *Schnaderhüpferl*,* casually interspersing a few snatches of the cheerful melody. A happy mood settled over the little group.

"Who composed such pretty songs?" asked Elisabeth.

"That's easy to guess," said Erich: "barbers, tailors' apprentices and other light-hearted folk."

"But they are not composed," said Reinhard, "they just grow, or fall from the sky, and spread hither and thither over the countryside like gossamer. People sing them in a thousand different places at the same time, expressing in them man's most personal thoughts and deeds. It is as though we have all taken part in their making."

Picking up another, he read:

"I stood upon a mountain top..."

"I know that one!" cried Elisabeth. "Come on, Reinhard, I'll sing it with you!"

And together, Elisabeth singing the descant in her soft contralto voice, they sang that melody which sounds so mysterious that it seems hardly to be the creation of human minds.

Elisabeth's mother was busy with her needlework, while Erich folded his hands and listened devotedly

When they had finished, Reinhard put the music away without a word.

The sound of cowbells floated up from the lakeshore on the stillness of the evening air, and as they listened they heard the ringing tones of a boy's voice:

"I stood upon a mountain top
And saw the depths below..."

"You see?" smiled Reinhard as he listened. "These songs live on."

"We often hear singing in these parts," said Elisabeth.

"It's the boy driving the cattle home," added Erich.

They listened until the sound of the bells finally died away behind the farm buildings on the hillside.

"Those are the sounds of primeval nature," said Reinhard. "They come from the depths of the earth, and no one knows who invented them."

He picked out another sheet from the pile.

The sun was setting, and a hazy red glow settled over the woods beyond the lake. Reinhard unrolled the manuscript. Elisabeth held one side of it in her hand, and they looked at it together as Reinhard read:

> "My mother wished it so,
> Yet it was not my will
> That I should leave the love I had,
> Surrender to another lad,
> And bid my heart be still.
>
> My mother bears the blame
> For my unhappy state:
> The things that should bring joy in life
> Have nurtured shame and guilt and strife –
> But now it is too late.
>
> All pride and joy is gone,
> And anguish fills my mind.
> Would that I could forget my pain,
> Could wander through the world again
> And leave my cares behind!"

Reinhard felt the sheet tremble us he read, and when he had finished, Elisabeth rose from her chair and went out silently into the garden, watched by her mother. Erich was on the point of following her, but her mother held him back.

"Elisabeth has some things to attend to outside," she said. So he let her go.

Outside the darkness was closing in around the lake and the garden, moths fluttered past the open doors through which the scent of flowers and bushes was wafted in; from the water came the sound of the croaking of frogs, and as the moon rose, the song of nightingales was heard, one from beneath the windows and another in the distance. For a long while he stared at the bushes through which the frail figure of Elisabeth had passed, then rolled up his manuscript, took his leave of the others and left the house in the direction of the lake.

The woods were silent, casting their dark shadow far out over the water, while the centre of the lake was illuminated by the pale moonlight. From time to time the leaves rustled, but there was no wind – only the gentle breath of the mild summer night.

Reinhard walked by the side of the water. Within a stone's throw of the bank he caught sight of a white water lily and suddenly felt an urge to see it from close quarters.

Taking off his clothes, he entered the water. Plants and sharp stones stung his feet, and it was too shallow to swim. Then suddenly the ground sloped away; the waters swirled over his head, and it took him some time to fight his way to the surface.

He swam around a little until he had gained his bearings, then, catching a glimpse of the lily as it lay between the broad, shining leaves, he swam out slowly towards it, the moonlight shining on the drops of water that fell from his glistening arms as he propelled himself forwards. But the distance between him and the lily never seemed to change, whilst the bank behind him became more and more indistinct. Yet he had no thought of turning back, and swam with powerful strokes towards the middle.

At length he came close enough to the flower to be able to distinguish its silver leaves in the moonlight, but as he did so, he felt as though he were becoming entangled in a net: the smooth stems stretched up from the bottom of the lake and twined themselves around his naked limbs. The black waters swirled around mysteriously, and he heard a fish leap up behind him. In a fit of panic he tore the clinging tendrils savagely from his body and struck out feverishly for the bank. When he finally reached it and looked back across the water, the lily was still floating there above the distant murky depths.

He put on his clothes and walked slowly homewards. As he entered the drawing room from the garden, he found Erich and Elisabeth's mother making arrangements for a short business trip the following day.

"Where have you been at this time of the night?" she cried as she caught sight of Reinhard.

"Where have I been?" he repeated. "Why, I wanted to visit the water lily, but I found that it could not be done."

"Who can be expected to believe that?" said Erich. "How in Heaven's name can one visit a water lily?"

"I once knew her," answered Reinhard, "but that was a long while ago."

Elisabeth

The following afternoon Reinhard and Elisabeth went for a stroll on the far side of the lake, sometimes passing through wooded copses, sometimes walking along the raised bank by the water's edge. Erich had told Elisabeth that, while her mother and he were away, she should show Reinhard the most attractive views of the surrounding landscape, in particular those of the house itself from the other side of the lake.

They walked from one place to another. At last Elisabeth became tired; she sat down in the shade of the overhanging branches, while Reinhard leant against a tree opposite her. A cuckoo called from the depths of the forest – and suddenly he had the feeling that he had lived this scene before. Looking at her with a strange smile, he said:

"Shall we go and look for strawberries?"

"This is not the season for strawberries," she replied.

"But it soon will be."

Elisabeth shook her head without speaking. Then she stood up, and they walked on. Time and again he glanced at the figure tripping gracefully at his side as though she were borne along by her clothes, and often he held back so as to look deep into her eyes.

They came to a grass-covered clearing from which they could see far out into the countryside. Reinhard bent down and picked some of the plants that were growing there. When he looked up, he showed pain and anguish in his face.

"Do you recognize this flower?" he murmured.

She looked at him in surprise.

"It's heather. I've often picked it in the woods."

"I have an old book at home," he said, "in which, a long while ago, I used to write down all kinds of poems and rhymes. There is heather – a faded one – pressed between its pages. Do you know who gave it to me?"

She nodded silently, casting her eyes down and looking only at the little flower that he held in his hand. For a long time they stood there, motionless. When at last she raised her head, he saw that her eyes were filled with tears.

"Our childhood lies beyond those mountains, Elisabeth," he said softly. "What has happened to it?"

They both fell silent and walked on side by side towards the lake. The air was humid, and dark clouds were gathering in the west.

"There's going to be a storm," said Elisabeth, quickening her step.

Reinhard nodded. They hurried along the bank until they reached the spot where they had left their boat.

As Reinhard pulled at the oars, she let her hand rest on the side of the boat. He looked towards her, but she stared past him into the distance. He lowered his gaze, and his eyes came to rest on her hand. This pale hand, resting on the boat, told him all that her face had withheld from him; subtly but plainly it betrayed, as a beautiful hand so often will, the heart that suffers secretly in the loneliness of the night. When she noticed him looking at it, she let it slip slowly over the side of the boat into the water.

As they walked up to the house, they saw a knife-grinder's cart. A man with long black hair was busily operating the treadle, humming a gypsy song as he did so, while his dog, chained to the cart, slept by his side. At the entrance to the yard stood a tattered beggar girl with fine but haggard features, who stretched out her hand imploringly to Elisabeth.

Reinhard put his hand in his pocket, but before he could find something to give her, Elisabeth hastily emptied the entire contents of her purse into the beggar girl's hand. Then she turned away abruptly, and Reinhard heard her sobbing as she went up the steps into the house. He wanted to stop her, then changed his mind and stayed at the foot of the steps. The beggar-girl was still standing there, motionless, clasping the money in her hands.

"What else do you want?" demanded Reinhard.

She gave a start.

"Nothing," she stammered, and walked slowly towards the gate, staring back at him with her fiery eyes as she went. He shouted something at her but she was out of earshot, and with bowed head, her arms folded, she passed out of the yard.

> But at my death
> I shall suffer alone.

The strains of the old song sounded in his ears, and his heart stood still. Then he turned away and went up to his room.

He sat down and tried to work, but his mind was a blank and after half-an-hour's fruitless effort he went down into the drawing room. The room was empty; only the evening sunlight shone in through the overhanging foliage. On Elisabeth's bureau there lay a red scarf that she had been wearing that afternoon. He picked it up, but it hurt his hand and he put it back quickly.

Seized by a sudden restlessness, he left the house and went down to the lake. Untying the boat, he rowed over to the other side and retraced all the paths along which he had walked with Elisabeth earlier in the day.

By the time he got back, it was dark. Elisabeth's mother and Erich had just returned, and as he crossed the courtyard, the coachman passed him, leading the horses out to graze. Entering the hall, he heard Erich walking up and down in the drawing room; he did not go in but paused for a moment, then went quietly up the stairs to his room.

He sat down in the armchair by the window and tried to listen to the throbbing music of the nightingale in the hedges below. But all he could hear was the beat of his own heart. Everybody else in the house had gone to bed.

The night wore on, and still he sat there. At last, hours later, he rose from the chair and lay down in front of the open window. The dew had settled on the leaves, and the nightingale was no longer singing. Slowly the deep blue of the night sky gave way to a pale yellow glow from the east, and a cold breeze caressed his fevered brow. The first lark flew upwards, singing joyously.

Reinhard turned away abruptly and walked across to his desk. He felt for a pencil, sat down and wrote a few lines on a sheet of paper.

Then, leaving the paper on the desk, he got up, took his hat and cane, opened the door softly and went downstairs.

Everything was still. The big cat stretched itself on the mat and arched its back as he bent down to stroke it. In the garden the sparrows were proclaiming to all and sundry that the night was past.

He heard a door open and the sound of footsteps on the stairs. Looking up, he found Elisabeth standing in front of him. She put her hand on his arm and her lips moved, but no sound came from them. At last she said:

"Do not deceive me, Reinhard. I know you will never come back."

"Never," he repeated.

She drew her hand away and was silent. He walked across the yard towards the gate, then stopped and looked back. She was standing motionless at the same spot, staring blankly after him. He took a step forwards and stretched out his arms towards her. Then he turned quickly on his heel and went out of the gate.

Outside the world was bathed in the glow of morning, and the dewdrops in the spiders' webs glistened in the early sunlight.

He did not look back. As he walked swiftly on, the house and the farm buildings grew smaller and smaller, while before him stretched the great wide world...

The Old Man

The moon was no longer shining through the window and it had become dark. But still the old man sat in his chair, his hands folded in front of him, and gazed across the room. As he looked, the darkness slowly gave way to the dark waters of a lake; it grew gradually wider and deeper, and at its furthest point, so distant that he could barely see it, there floated a solitary white water lily, nestling between broad green leaves.

The door opened and a bright ray of light shone into the room.

"I am glad you have come, Brigitte," he said. "Put the lamp on the table."

Then he drew up his chair to the table, picked up one of the open books and engrossed himself in subjects to which he had devoted himself in the days of his youth.

Part Two

Viola Tricolor
and
Curator Carsten

Introduction to Viola Tricolor and Curator Carsten

HANS THEODOR WOLDSEN STORM was born in 1817 at Husum, a town of about four thousand inhabitants on the west coast of Schleswig, as the son of well-to-do and substantial people. He studied law at Kiel and Berlin, at the same time writing poetry, browsing widely in German literature, and forming friendships with men of literary interests. His first publication was a volume of poetry issued in collaboration with Tycho and Theodor Mommsen.

Beginning the practice of law in Husum, Storm soon met a cousin, Constanze Esmarch, whom he married in 1846. Seven of Constanze's children survived, but she died shortly after the last birth, in 1865.

Meanwhile Schleswig had been annexed by Denmark in 1851. As Storm remained loyal to Germany, his licence to practise was annulled in 1852, whereupon he took his family into voluntary exile in Prussia, which lasted until Prussia recovered his homeland in 1864. On returning to Husum, he became its mayor, but in 1867 he gave up this post and was made circuit judge of the Husum district, an office which he retained until his retirement in 1880.

The death of Constanze made it almost imperative for Storm to remarry, as his children needed a mother's care. His second wife, Doris Jensen, who had long been devoted to him, found herself in a problematic situation as regards the children, and Storm himself increased her difficulties in the beginning, so that she lapsed into melancholia, which she was long in overcoming.

Storm spent the years after his retirement in the village of Hademarschen, where he died in 1888.

As a writer, Storm became a master of the shorter forms of narrative fiction, of which he published more than fifty of widely varying length; he is also regarded as a lyric poet of exceptionally high quality. His most admired stories include *Immensee, Pole Poppenspäler, Psyche, Aquis submersus, Renate, Eekenhof, Zur Chronik von Grieshuus* and *Der Schimmelreiter.*

"Viola tricolor" is the botanical name for the wild pansy, commonly called in German *Stiefmütterchen* (little stepmother). In this touching story, the widespread conception of the cruel and evil stepmother is countered by a sensitive portrait of a second wife who is eager to love her stepdaughter and has to overcome the latter's initial hostility and aloofness. While not strictly autobiographical, the story undoubtedly draws on the spiritual problems which Doris Storm, with her husband's belated help, finally succeeded in solving.

Curator Carsten makes use of a more sombre autobiographical element. Storm's oldest son, whom he had adored as a child and youth (and probably spoilt), turned out to be completely unprincipled, and on reaching maturity he became a drunkard. It is clear that in many respects Carsten's relation to Heinrich parallels that of the author to his son Hans. The tragic end is no mere conventional affair: it reflects the poet's firm conviction, a by-product of Darwinian speculations, that there is no salvation but death for a person whose heredity condemns him to a frustrated life. At the same time, Storm makes effective use of the North Sea, which he knew and loved in all its aspects.

While these two stories do not show Storm at the height of his artistry, they are rated among those on which his reputation is firmly based.

– Bayard Quincy Morgan

Viola Tricolor

The Little Stepmother

Translated by Bayard Quincy Morgan

I T WAS VERY STILL in the great house, but even in the hall one detected the scent of fresh flowers.

Out of one of the double doors which faced the broad stairway leading to the upper storey stepped a neatly dressed old serving woman. With a solemn air of self-satisfaction she latched the door behind her and then let her grey eyes rove along the walls, as if she would subject every speck of dust to a final inspection, but she nodded her approval and then cast a glance at the old English clock, whose chime had just played its second theme.

"Already half past!" murmured she. "And at eight, so the Professor wrote, they were expecting to be here!"

Hereupon she reached into her pocket for a big bunch of keys and then disappeared in the rear of the house. And again it grew still; only the tick of the pendulum sounded through the spacious hall and up the staircase; through the window above the front door a ray of evening sunshine came in and gleamed on the three gilt knobs which surmounted the clock case.

Then short, light steps came down the stairs, and a girl of about ten years appeared on the landing. She too was freshly and festally attired; the red-and-white striped dress was becoming to her olive complexion and her glossy black braids. She laid her arm on the banister and her head on her arm and let herself slowly slide downward, while her dark eyes were dreamily directed to the opposite doorway.

For a moment she stood listening in the hall; then she softly opened the door of the room and slipped in through the heavy portières. Here it was already dim, for the two windows of the long room opened on a street hemmed in by tall houses; only to one side above the sofa a Venetian mirror gleamed like silver on the dark-green velvet wall-covering. In this solitude it seemed meant to reflect the image of a fresh bouquet of roses, which stood in a marble vase on the table by the sofa. But soon the dark head of the child also appeared in its frame. On her toes the little one had crept up over the soft carpet, and already the slender fingers were hastily reaching in among the flower stems, while her eyes sped back towards the door. Finally she had succeeded in lifting a half-open rosebud out of the bouquet, but in her zeal she had not thought of the thorns, and a red drop of blood trickled down her arm. Quickly – for it had almost fallen on the pattern of the precious table cover – she sucked it up with her lips; then as softly as she had come, with the stolen rose in her hand, she again slipped through the portières out into the hall. After she had once more stopped to listen, she again flew up the stairs that she had just descended, and she went along a corridor until she reached the last door. She cast one more glance through one of the windows, before which the swallows were criss-crossing in the afterglow; then she lifted the latch.

It was her father's study, which she was otherwise not wont to enter during his absence; now she was quite alone among the tall cases, which stood about so awe-inspiringly with their countless books. When she had hesitantly latched the door behind her, the mighty baying of a dog was heard under one of the windows to the left of it. A smile flitted over the serious features of the child; she swiftly went to the window and looked out. Below her the great garden of the house spread out in broad patches of lawn and shrubbery, but her four-legged friend seemed already to have gone other ways; sharply as she peered, there was nothing to be seen. And something like a shadow again descended upon the face of the child; she had come here for a different purpose; what did Nero matter to her now!

Towards the west, opposite the door through which she had entered, the room had a second window. Against the wall next to it, so that the light fell on the hand of him who sat at it, stood a great writing desk with all the apparatus of a learned archaeologist: bronzes and terracottas from Rome and Greece, little models of ancient temples and houses, and other articles risen up out of the debris of the past, filled almost the entire top-piece. But above it, as if emerging from blue spring air, hung the life-size head of a young woman; like a youthful crown the gold-blonde braids lay about the clear brow. "Beauteous", this antiquated word had been revived for her by her friends long ago, when she was still wont to greet with her smile those who crossed the threshold of this house. And so she looked down from the wall even now in this portrait, with her blue child-eyes; only about the mouth there played a slight trace of melancholy, which no one had seen on her in life. At the time the painter had no doubt been rebuked for it; later, after she had died, all seemed reconciled to it.

The little black-haired girl approached with soft steps; with passionate intensity her eyes clung to the lovely portrait.

"Mother, my mother!" she said in a whisper, but as if she were trying to reach her with the words.

The beautiful face looked down lifelessly from the wall, as before, but the child climbed, nimble as a cat, over the chair upon the desk, and now stood with defiantly curling lips before the picture, while her trembling hands tried to fasten the stolen rose behind the lower bar of the gold frame. When she had achieved this, she got down again quickly and with her handkerchief carefully wiped the marks of her feet from the desktop.

But now it seemed as if she could not find her way out of the room that she had previously entered so timidly; after she had already taken some steps towards the door, she turned about again; the west window beside the desk seemed to exert this attraction upon her.

Here too there was a garden down below, or, to be more exact, a garden wilderness. The space to be sure was small, for where the rampant shrubs did not cover the high surrounding wall, it was visible on every side. Against this wall, opposite the window, there was an open reed hut in evident dilapidation; in front of it, almost covered by the green fabric of a clematis, stood a garden chair. Facing the hut there must once have been a clump of standard roses, but now they hung like dry twigs on the faded stalks, while below them, covered with countless blooms, cabbage roses scattered their falling petals all about on grass and weeds.

The little girl had propped her arms on the window sill and her chin on her two hands, and looked down with eyes of longing.

Two swallows were flying in and out of the reed hut; they must have built their nest inside it. The other birds had already gone to rest; only a redbreast was still singing lustily from the topmost branch of the denuded laburnum, looking at the child with his black eyes.

"Aggie, where are you keeping yourself?" said an old voice gently, while a hand laid itself caressingly on the head of the child.

The old serving woman had come in unnoticed. The child turned her head and looked at her with a weary expression. "Annie," she said, "I do wish I could go into grandmother's garden again!"

The old woman did not answer; she merely pressed her lips together and nodded a couple of times as if agreeing. "Come, come!" she then said. "How you look! They'll be here right away, your father and your new mother!" With that she drew the child into her arms and put hair and dress in order with stroking, twitching fingers. "No, no, Aggie! You mustn't cry; they say she is a kind lady, and pretty, Aggie, and you like to look at handsome people!"

At this moment the rattle of a carriage came up to them from the street. The child started, but Anna took her by the hand and quickly pulled her out of the room. They were in time to see the carriage drive up; the two maids had already opened the front door.

The old servant's statement seemed to be justified. A man of about forty years, in whose serious features one could easily recognize Aggie's father, lifted a beautiful young woman out of the carriage. Her hair and eyes were almost as dark as those of the child whose stepmother she had become; indeed at a fleeting glance one might have taken her for the child's own mother, had she not been too young for that. She bowed graciously, her eyes looking about as if seeking something, but her husband led her quickly into the house and into the downstairs room, where she was greeted by the fresh scent of roses.

"Here we shall live together," he said, as he forced her down into a soft armchair, "do not leave this room without having found your first moment of rest in your new home!"

She looked up at him confidingly. "But you, will you not stay with me?"

"I will bring to you the best treasure of our house."

"Yes, yes, Rudolf, your Agnes! Where was she just now?"

He had already left the room. It had not escaped the father's eyes that at their arrival Aggie had kept hidden behind old Annie; now, finding her standing out in the hall as if lost, he lifted her up in his two arms and carried her thus into the room.

"And here you have Aggie!" he said, laying the child on the rug at the feet of her lovely stepmother; then, as if he had other things to attend to, he went out; he wanted to let these two find the way to each other.

Aggie slowly got herself up and stood in silence before the young wife; they looked each other in the eye, uncertain and guarded. The latter, who had undoubtedly assumed a friendly reception as a matter of course, finally grasped the hands of the little girl and said gravely,

"You know I'm your mother now, so shan't we love each other, Agnes?"

Aggie looked at the floor.

"But I may say Mama?" she asked timidly.

"Of course, Agnes; call me what you like, Mama or Mother, just as you prefer!"

The child looked up at her in embarrassment and replied anxiously, "I could say Mama easily!"

The young woman cast a quick glance at her, then fixed her dark eyes on the still darker ones of the child. "Mama, but not Mother?" she asked.

"My mother is dead," said Aggie softly.

In an involuntary agitation the young woman's hands pushed the child away, but immediately she drew it back passionately to her breast.

"Aggie," she said, "Mother and Mama is the same thing!"

But Aggie made no reply; she had never called her own mother anything but Mother.

The conversation was at an end. The father had come in again, and finding his little daughter in the arms of his young wife, he smiled contentedly.

"But come now," he said cheerily, as he held out his hand to the latter, "and as mistress take possession of all the rooms in the house!"

And they went out together; through the downstairs rooms, through kitchen and cellar, then up the broad stairs into a great hall and into the smaller rooms which opened into the corridor on both sides of the stairs.

The dark of evening had already fallen; the young wife hung more and more heavily on the arm of her husband; it almost seemed that with every door which opened before her a new load rested on her shoulders; ever briefer grew the replies to his happy and fluent speeches. At last, when they were standing before the door of his study, he too was silent and raised the lovely head, which rested mutely on his shoulder, up to his own.

"What is it, Inez?" he said. "You are not glad!"

"O yes, I am glad!"

"Then come!"

As he opened the door, a soft light shone upon them. Through the west window shone the gleam of the golden sunset, coming from beyond the shrubs of the little garden. In this light the lovely picture of the dead woman looked down from the wall; below it on the dull gold of the frame the fresh red rose lay like a flame.

Involuntarily the young wife laid her hand upon her heart and stared speechless at the sweet lifelike picture. But already the arms of her husband had firmly embraced her.

"She was once my happiness," he said. "Now it is to be you!"

She nodded, but without speaking, struggling for breath. Oh, this dead wife was still alive, and for both of them there could not be room in one house!

Just as before, when Aggie had been here, from the great north garden came the mighty baying of a dog.

With gentle hand the young wife was led by her husband to the north window. "Look down there a moment!" he said.

Down below on the path which encircled the wide lawn sat a black Newfoundland dog; before him stood Aggie, describing with one of her black braids an ever narrowing circle around his nose. Then the dog threw back his head and barked, and Aggie laughed and began the game all over again.

The father too, as he looked on at this childish play, had to smile, but the young woman at his side did not smile, and it was as if a dark cloud floated over him. "If it were her mother!" he thought, but aloud he said, "That is our Nero, you must get acquainted with him too, Inez; he and Aggie are good comrades, and the huge beast will even let himself be harnessed to her doll carriage."

She looked up at him. "There is so much here, Rudolf," she said half absently. "If I can only find my way through it all!"

"Inez, you are dreaming! Just ourselves and the child, it is the smallest family to be found."

"To be found?" she repeated dully, and her eyes followed the child, who was now racing around the lawn with the dog; then suddenly, looking up at her husband as if in fear, she threw her arms about his neck and pleaded, "Hold me tight, help me! I feel so heavy-hearted."

Weeks and months went by. The fears of the young wife seemed not to materialize; the household seemed to run itself under her management. The servants submitted readily to her rule, at once friendly and dignified, and all those who came in from outside felt that the master's house was once more in the hands of a wife who was a proper match for him. The keener eyes of the husband, to be sure, saw things differently; he recognized only too clearly that she dealt with the things of his house as if she had no part in them, but must look after them all the more conscientiously, as a mere caretaker. It could not reassure this experienced man that at times she would nestle up to him with passionate intensity, as if she must assure herself that she belonged to him, and he to her.

Nor had a closer relationship to Aggie developed. An inner voice, both of love and of wisdom, urged the young woman to talk to the child about her mother, the memory of whom she had preserved so vividly, so obstinately, ever since her stepmother had entered the house. But that was just the trouble! The sweet picture which hung upstairs in her husband's room, even the eyes of her mind refrained from looking at it. She had indeed plucked up courage more than once; she had drawn the child to her with both hands, but then had lapsed into silence; her lips had failed her, and Aggie, whose dark eyes had lit up joyously at such a heartfelt impulse, had sadly gone away again. For strange to say, she was longing for the love of this beautiful woman, in fact, as children will, she secretly worshipped her. But she lacked a form of address, which is the key to every cordial conversation; the one form, so she felt, she might use, the other she could not use.

This latter hindrance was felt by Inez too, and since it seemed the easiest to remove, her thoughts reverted to the point again and again.

So she was sitting one afternoon beside her husband in the living room, looking into the steam which arose with a soft hum from the tea kettle.

Rudolf, who had just finished looking through the newspaper, took her hand. "You are so still, Inez; today you didn't interrupt me a single time!"

"There's something I'd like to say," she replied hesitantly, freeing her hand from his.

"Say it then!"

But still she was silent awhile.

"Rudolf," she said at last, "tell your child to call me Mother!"

"Why, doesn't she do that?"

She shook her head and told him what had happened on the day of her arrival.

He listened quietly. "It is an expedient," he then said, "that the child's soul unconsciously discovered all by itself. Shall we not be thankful for it?"

The young wife did not answer the question, she merely said, "Then the child will never come close to me."

Again he tried to take her hand, but she withheld it.

"Inez," he said, "you must not demand what nature denies; don't require of Aggie that she be your child, nor of yourself that you be her mother!"

Tears burst from her eyes. "But – I am supposed to be her mother," she said almost vehemently.

"Her mother? No, Inez, that's not expected of you."

"Then what is expected, Rudolf?"

Had she been able to understand the obvious reply to this question, she would have given it herself. He felt that and looked thoughtfully into her eyes, as if he must look there for the helping words.

"Admit it now!" she said, misinterpreting his silence, "you have no answer to that."

"O Inez!" he cried. "Wait until a child of your own blood lies in your lap!"

She made a gesture of rejection, but he went on, "The time will come, and you will feel how the delight that radiates from your eyes will awaken the first smile of your child and draw its little soul to you. Over Aggie, too, two blissful eyes once shone like that; then she would throw her little arm about a neck that stooped down to her, and would say, 'Mother.' Don't be angry at her for being unable to say that to any other woman in the world!"

Inez had scarcely heard his words; her thoughts were following only the one point. "If you can say: She is not your child, then why don't you also say: You are not my wife!"

And there the matter rested. What did she care about his arguments!

He drew her to him; he tried to quiet her; she kissed him and smiled at him through her tears, but it did not solve her problem.

When Rudolf had left her, she went out into the great garden. Upon entering it she saw Aggie with a schoolbook in her hand walking around the wide lawn, but she avoided her and took a side-path that led between bushes and along the garden wall.

The expression of sadness in the lovely eyes of her stepmother had not escaped the child's fleeting glimpse of her, and as if drawn by a magnet, still studying and murmuring her lesson out loud, she too had gradually got upon that path.

Inez was just standing before a gate in the high wall, which was almost covered up by a climbing plant with lavender blossoms. Her eyes rested absently upon it, and she was just about to resume her quiet stroll when she saw the child coming towards her.

Now she stood still and asked, "What gate is this, Aggie?"

"To grandmother's garden!"

"To grandmother's garden? Why, your grandparents have been dead for a long time!"

"Oh yes, a long, long time."

"And whose is the garden now?"

"It's ours!" said the child, as if that were a matter of course.

Inez bent her head under the branches and began to pull and shake the iron latch of the door; Aggie stood by in silence, as if waiting to see the result of these efforts.

"But it is locked!" said the young wife, as she desisted and wiped the rust from her fingers with her handkerchief. "Is it that neglected garden that one can see from father's study window?"

The child nodded.

"Listen, hear how the birds are singing over there."

Meanwhile old Anna had entered the garden. When she heard the two voices by the wall, she hastened to join them. "There are callers inside," she reported.

Inez laid her hand kindly on Aggie's cheek. "Father is a poor gardener," she said as she moved away. "We two must get in there and set things to rights."

In the house Rudolf came to meet her.

"You know that the Müller quartet is playing tonight," he said. "The doctor and his wife are here to warn us against sins of omission."

When they had joined the visitors in the parlour, a long and animated conversation about music ensued; then there were household affairs to be attended to. For this day the neglected garden was forgotten.

In the evening the concert was given. The great past masters, Haydn and Mozart, had swept by the listeners, and now the last chord of Beethoven's C minor quartet was dying away, and in place of the solemn stillness in which only the musical notes gleamed up and down, the chatter of the crowding audience filled the spacious room.

Rudolf stood beside the chair of his young wife. "It is over, Inez," he said, bending over her. "Or do you still keep on hearing something?"

She still sat as if listening, her eyes directed to the platform, on which nothing but the empty stands remained. Now she held out her hand to her husband. "Let us go home, Rudolf," she said, getting up.

At the door they were stopped by their physician and his wife, the only persons with whom Inez had so far formed any close association.

"Well?" said the doctor, nodding to them with the expression of the deepest contentment. "But come along with us, our house is right on your way; after a concert like this one should stay together for a while."

Rudolf was just about to express a cheerful acceptance when he felt his sleeve gently plucked and saw the eyes of his wife fixed upon him in the most urgent pleading. He understood her perfectly. "I refer the decision to a higher court," he said humorously.

And Inez inflexibly managed to put off the doctor, not so easily overcome, to another evening.

When they had taken leave of these friends at their own house, she drew a deep breath of liberation.

"What do you have against our nice doctor and his wife?" Rudolf asked.

She nestled tightly into his arm. "Nothing," said she, "but it was so beautiful this evening; I must be quite alone with you."

They quickened their homeward pace.

"Look," he said, "there is a light in the downstairs room; old Annie has no doubt got the tea-table ready. You were right; it is better to be at home than with others."

She merely nodded and quietly pressed his hand. Then they entered their house; quickly she opened the parlour door and pushed back the curtains.

On the table where the vase of roses had once stood a great bronze lamp was now burning, lighting up the head of a black-haired child which had drooped in sleep upon her thin little arms; the corners of a picture-book stuck out beneath them.

The young wife stood in the doorway as if petrified; the child had disappeared entirely from the sphere of her thoughts. A trace of bitter disappointment flitted about her pretty lips. "You, Aggie!" she managed to say, when her husband had led her fully into the room. "What are you doing here?"

Aggie awoke and jumped up. "I wanted to wait for you," she said, half smiling and passing her hand over her blinking eyes.

"That was wrong of Annie; you should have been in bed long ago."

Inez turned away and went to the window; she felt the tears welling up out of her eyes. A mass of bitter feelings swirled in her breast, beyond disentangling; homesickness, self-pity, regret for her lovelessness towards the child of the beloved man; she herself did not know how much came over her now, but, and with the voluptuousness and the injustice of pain she stated it to herself, this was it: her marriage lacked youth, and yet she herself was still so young!

When she turned around, the room was empty. Where was the nice hour she had looked forward to? It did not occur to her that she herself had spoilt it.

The child, who had witnessed with almost frightened eyes this to her incomprehensible happening, had been quietly led away by her father.

"Patience!" he said to himself, as he went up the stairs with Aggie, his arm embracing her, and he too, though in another sense, added: "She is still so young."

A whole series of ideas and plans arose in him; mechanically he opened the door of the room where Aggie slept with old Annie, and where the latter was already expecting her. He kissed her and said, "I will say good night to Mama for you." Then he was about to go down to his wife, but he turned around again and went into his study at the end of the corridor.

On the desktop stood a small bronze lamp from Pompeii, which he had but recently acquired and experimentally filled with oil; he took it down, lit it, and replaced it under the portrait of the deceased;

a glass with flowers in it, which had been standing on the desk, he stood beside the lamp. He did this almost without thinking; only as if he must give his hands something to do while his head and heart were engaged. Then he stepped up to the adjacent window and opened both casements.

The sky was full of clouds; the light of the moon could not get through. Down below in the little garden the rampant shrubbery looked like one dark mass; only over yonder, where the path led to the reed hut through the black pyramids of the conifers, the white gravel shimmered between them.

And out of the man's imagination, as he looked down into this solitude, issued a lovely figure which no longer belonged among the living; he saw her walking on the path below, and it seemed to him that he was walking at her side.

"Let the memory of you strengthen me for loving," he said, but the dead woman gave no answer; she kept her lovely pale face inclined towards the earth; with a sweet shuddering he felt her nearness, but no words came from her.

Now he recalled that he was standing up here all alone. He believed in the full seriousness of death; the time when she had been was now past. But below him lay the garden of her parents, as it had always been; looking up from his books and through the window, it was there that he had first seen the girl, then scarcely fifteen years old, and the child with the blonde braids had carried off the thoughts of the serious man, more and more, until at last she had crossed the threshold of his house as wife, bringing back to him all this and more. Years of happiness and of joyful productiveness had entered in with her, but when her parents had died and their house was sold, they had kept the little garden and had united it by means of a gate in the boundary wall with their own great garden. Even at that time this gate was almost hidden under overhanging bushes, which they allowed to grow unchecked; for they walked through it into the most intimate spot of their summer life, to which even their best friends were but rarely admitted.

In the reed hut, in which he had once watched from his window the youthful sweetheart doing her schoolwork, there now sat a child with dark, thoughtful eyes at the feet of her blonde mother, and whenever he turned his head away from his work, he enjoyed a glimpse into the fullest happiness of human life. But death had secretly sown his seed there. It was in the first days of June that they bore the bed of the gravely ailing wife from the adjoining bedroom to the study of her husband; she wanted to keep about her the air that blew into the open window from the garden of her happiness. The great desk was pushed to one side; all his thoughts were now with her. Outside an incomparable spring had come to life; a cherry tree stood there snowed in with bloom. In an involuntary urge he lifted the slight figure from the bed and carried her to the window.

"Oh, just look at it! How lovely the world is!"

But she gently rocked her head, saying, "I don't see it any more."

And soon it had come to the point where he could no longer interpret the whispers that came from her lips. Fainter and fainter gleamed the spark; only a painful twitching stirred the lips, the breath came with harsh groaning in the battle for life. But it grew softer and ever softer, at last as gentle as the hum of a bee. Then for one last time it was as if a blue ray of light passed through the open eyes, and then came peace.

"Good night, Marie!" But she was beyond hearing.

One day more, and the silent, noble figure lay downstairs in its coffin in the large dim room. The servants walked about softly; he stood inside next to his child, whom old Annie was holding by the hand.

"Aggie," said the latter, "you're not afraid, I hope?"

And the child, touched by the exaltation of death, answered, "No, Annie, I am praying."

Then came the final journey, the last he was permitted to take with her; without priest or the peal of bells, as they had both willed it, but in the holiness of early morning, as the first larks were mounting high in the air.

That was over now, but he still possessed her in his grief; though unseen, she still lived with him. But this too faded away unnoticed; he often sought her in terror, but less and less often could he manage to find her. Now his house did indeed seem to him weirdly empty and desolate; in the corners dwelt an obscurity which had never been there before; all about him was so strangely different, and she was nowhere.

The moon had come out from behind the cloud-banks and was brightly illuminating the garden wilderness below. He was still standing at the same spot, his head resting against the window bars, but his eyes no longer saw what was outside.

Then the door opened behind him, and a dark and beautiful woman came in.

The soft rustle of her dress had found its way to his ear; he turned his head and looked searchingly at her.

"Inez!" he cried; the tone was impetuous, but he did not go towards her.

She had stopped short. "What ails you, Rudolf? Do I startle you?"

He shook his head and tried to smile. "Come," said he, "let us go downstairs."

But as he took her hand her eyes had fallen upon the picture lit up by the lamp and the flowers close by.

Her features revealed a sudden flash of understanding.

"Your room is like a chapel," she said, and her words sounded cold, almost hostile.

He had understood everything. "O Inez," he cried, "are not the dead sacred to you too?"

"The dead! Who would not keep them sacred! But Rudolf," and she drew him back to the window; her hands trembled and her black eyes flickered with agitation, "tell me, who am now your wife, why do you keep this garden locked up and never let any human foot enter it?"

He pointed downward; the white gravel between the black shrub-pyramids had a ghostly gleam; a great night moth was just flying across it.

He had looked down in silence. "That is a grave, Inez," he said now, "or, if you prefer, a garden of the past."

But she looked at him with passion. "I know better, Rudolf! That is the place where you are with her; there on the white path you stroll together; for she is not dead; even now, in this very hour, you were with her and were accusing me, your wife, before her. That is unfaithfulness, Rudolf, you are committing adultery with a shadow!"

In silence he put his arm around her and led her, half by force, away from the window. Then he took the lamp from the desk and held it up to the picture. "Inez, take just one look at her!"

And as the innocent eyes of the dead girl looked down at her, she burst out in a flood of tears. "O Rudolf, I feel that I am growing wicked!"

"Do not weep so," said he. "I too have done wrong, but you must have patience with me, too!" He pulled out a drawer in his desk and laid a key in her hand. "Open up the garden again, Inez! Truly, it will make me happy if your foot is the first to re-enter it. Perhaps she will meet you there in spirit, and will look at you with her mild eyes so long that you will put your arm around her neck like a sister!"

She looked without moving at the key, which still lay on her open palm.

"Well, Inez, will you not accept what I have given you?"

She shook her head.

"Not yet, Rudolf, I can't just yet, but later – later; then we will go in there together." And as her lovely dark eyes looked pleadingly up at him, she quietly laid the key on the desk.

A seed-corn had been laid in the ground, but the time of germination was still remote.

It was in November. At last Inez could no longer doubt that she too was to become a mother, mother of her own child. But with the delight that came over her at this realization something else was soon associated. Something like an uncanny darkness lay over her, out of which, like an evil serpent, *one* thought gradually emerged. She tried to drive it away, she fled from it to all the good spirits of her house, but it pursued her, came again and again and in increasing power. Had she not merely entered this house externally and as a stranger, a house that already comprised a complete life-unit without her? And a second marriage, was there any such thing? Must not the first marriage, the only one, endure until the death of both? Not only until death! Further, too, further, to all eternity! And what then? The hot flush rushed to her face; lacerating her own flesh, she clutched at the harshest words. Her child – an intruder, a bastard in its own father's house!

She went about as if annihilated; she bore her young bliss and woe alone, and when he who had the best right to share it with her looked at her in question and concern, her lips closed as if in deadly fear.

In the conjugal chamber the heavy window shades were let down, and only through a narrow crack between them did a strip of moonlight steal in. Inez had fallen asleep amid torturing thoughts, and now the nightmare; now she knew; she could not stay, she must leave this house, taking only a small bundle with her, and then go, far away – to her mother, never to return! Out of the garden, behind the spruces which formed its rear wall, a gate led into the open; she had the key in her pocket, she would leave at once.

The moon moved forwards, from the bedstead to the pillow, and now her lovely countenance lay fully bathed in its pale gleam. She raised herself up. Noiselessly she got out of bed and put her bare feet into the shoes standing ready for her. Now she stood in the middle of her room in her white night robe; her dark hair hung over her breast in two long braids, as she was wont to do it at night. But her figure, usually so elastic, seemed to have shrunk; it was as if the burden of sleep were still resting upon her. Gropingly, with outstretched hands, she stole through the room, but she took nothing with her, no bundle, no key. As her fingers touched her husband's clothes lying on a chair, she hesitated for a moment, as if another idea were gaining ground in her mind, but immediately afterwards she stepped softly and solemnly out of the bedroom door and went down the stairs. In the hall below the front door lock clinked, cold air blew upon her, and the night wind lifted the heavy braids on her breast.

How she had got through the dark grove that lay behind her she did not know, but now she heard sounds bursting forth from the thicket on every side; the pursuers were behind her. In front of her rose up a great gate; with all the strength in her little hands she swung open one side of it; a desolate, endless heath spread out before her, and suddenly it was swarming with great black hounds, who were running towards her at full speed; she saw the red tongues hanging out of their steaming throats, she heard their baying come closer... louder...

Now her half closed eyes opened, and gradually she began to grasp the situation. She realized that she was standing inside the big garden; one of her hands was still holding the latch of the iron gate. The wind was playing with her light nightgown; from the lindens, which stood at one side of the entrance, a shower of yellow leaves whirled down upon her. But – what was that? From the fir trees over there, just as she had thought she was hearing it a moment before, came the baying of a hound at this moment, and she distinctly heard something bursting through the dry twigs. A mortal fear fell upon her. And again the baying resounded.

"Nero," said she, "it is Nero."

But she had never made friends with the black guardian of the house, and involuntarily she let the real animal fuse with the fierce beasts of her dream, and now she saw him bounding towards her in great leaps from the other side of the lawn. But he laid himself down before her, and with unmistakable whimpers of joy he licked her bare feet. At the same moment footsteps came towards her from the courtyard, and a moment later the arms of her husband were embracing her; in deep security she laid her head on his breast.

Aroused by the barking of the dog, he had looked at her place in the bed beside him in sudden fright and found it empty. Suddenly a dark pool gleamed before his mind's eye; it was on a country road only a thousand yards away from their garden under dense willows. He saw himself standing with Inez on its green bank, as they had done a few days before; he saw her going in among the reeds and throwing a stone she had picked up on the road into the deep water. "Come back, Inez!" he had called out, "it is not safe there." But she had remained standing, her melancholy eyes staring into the circles that slowly widened out on the black surface. "I suppose it is bottomless?" she had asked, when he finally snatched her away in his arms.

All this had raced wildly through his head as he dashed down the stairs to the courtyard. Then too they had left the house through the garden, and now he found her here, almost unclothed, her lovely hair moist with the night-dew which was still dripping from the trees.

He wrapped her in the shawl he had thrown over his own shoulder before coming down. "Inez," he said, his heart pounding so violently that he spoke almost roughly, "what is this? How did you get here?"

She shivered and shrank.

"I don't know, Rudolf. I wanted to leave. I had a dream. O Rudolf, it must have been something fearful!"

"You had a dream? Really, you had a dream!" he repeated, and he sighed deeply, as if freed from a heavy burden.

She merely nodded and let herself be led back into the house and bedroom like a child.

Then when he gently took his arms away, she said, "You are so silent, of course you are angry?"

"How should I be angry, Inez? I was afraid for you. Did you ever dream like that before?"

At first she shook her head, but then she thought again. "Yes I did once; only there was nothing terrible about it."

He stepped to the window and drew back the curtains, so that the moonlight streamed full into the room.

"I must see your face," he said, as he drew her down on the edge of her bed and then seated himself at her side. "Now will you tell me what nice things you dreamt that other time? You needn't speak loudly; in this delicate light even the softest sound strikes the ear."

She had laid her head on his breast and looked up at him.

"If you would like to know," she said, thinking back. "It was on my thirteenth birthday, I think; I had quite fallen in love with the Child, the little Jesus, and didn't want to look at my dolls any more."

"In love with little Jesus, Inez?"

"Yes, Rudolf," and she nestled still more tightly in his arm, as if to sleep there, "my mother had given me a picture, the Madonna with the Child; it hung in a pretty frame over my little work table in the living room."

"I know the one," he said, "it is still hanging there; your mother wanted to keep it as a memento of her little Inez."

"O my dear mother!"

He drew her more tightly to him; then he said, "May I hear some more, Inez?"

"Of course! But I am ashamed, Rudolf." And then continuing softly and hesitantly: "On that day I only had eyes for the Christ child; in the afternoon, too, when my playmates were there, I secretly crept up to it and kissed the glass over his little mouth. I felt just as if it were alive. I wished that I could take it in my arms like the mother in the picture!" She stopped; at the last words her voice had dropped to a mere whisper.

"And then, Inez?" he asked. "But you tell it so uneasily!"

"No, no, Rudolf! But in the night that followed I must have got up in my sleep; for on the next morning they found me in my bed fast asleep, with the picture in my arms, and my head on the broken glass."

For a while there was dead silence in the room.

"And now?" he asked with a dawning suspicion, looking deeply and warmly into her eyes. "What was it that drove you away from my side today and out into the night?"

"Now, Rudolf?" He felt a tremble course through all her limbs. Suddenly she flung her arms around his neck, and with stifled voice she whispered anxious and confused words, the sense of which he could not grasp.

"Inez, Inez!" he said, and took her lovely and mournful face in both his hands.

"O Rudolf! Let me die, but don't drive out our child!"

He had dropped on his knees before her and kissed her hands. He had heard only the message and not the ominous words in which it had been announced to him; all the shadows fled from his soul, and looking up at her hopefully, he said softly, "Now everything, everything must change for the better!" Time went on its way, but the dark powers were not yet overcome. Only with reluctance did Inez add to her own layette the things left from Aggie's babyhood, and many a tear fell on the little caps and jackets at which she now sewed silently and eagerly.

Aggie too had not failed to realize that something unusual was in prospect. On the second floor, a room that looked out on the big garden, in which her playthings had previously been kept, was suddenly kept locked; she had peeped through the keyhole; a sort of twilight seemed to dominate it, a solemn stillness. And when she carried her doll kitchen, which had been set out in the corridor, up into the attic with the help of old Annie, she looked there in vain for the cradle with the green taffeta shade, which had stood under the skylight in the roof as long as she could remember. She peered curiously into all the corners.

"What are you nosing around for like an inspector?" asked the old woman.

"Oh, well, Annie, I wonder what has become of my cradle?"

Annie looked at her with a sly smile. "What would you say," she said, "if the stork were to bring you a little brother?"

Aggie looked up in astonishment, but she felt her eleven-year-old dignity injured by this form of speech. "The stork?" she said contemptuously.

"That's right, Aggie."

"You mustn't say that to me, Annie. Little children believe that, but I know very well that it's nonsense."

"You do? If you know so much better, Little Miss Smarty, where do the children come from, if the stork doesn't bring them, as he's been doing all these thousands of years?"

"They come from God," said Aggie emotionally. "All of a sudden they're here."

"Now God preserve us!" cried the old woman. "How smart these little greenhorns are nowadays! But you are right, Aggie; if you are perfectly sure that God has discharged the stork from his office, I think so myself; He's able to manage it all alone. But now if all of a sudden he was here, that little brother (or would you rather have a little sister?) would you be glad, Aggie?"

Aggie stood in front of the old woman, who had let herself down on a big trunk; a smile lit up her grave little face, but then she seemed to be thinking it over.

"Well, Aggie," the old woman probed again. "Would you be glad, Aggie?"

"Yes, Annie," she said at last, "I'd like to have a little sister, and father would surely be glad too, but—"

"Well, Aggie, what are you butting about?"

"But," repeated Aggie, and then paused again for a moment as if puzzling over it, "then the poor child wouldn't have any mother!"

"What?" cried the old woman in great alarm, getting up laboriously from her trunk. "That child without a mother? You are too learned for me, Aggie; come, let's go downstairs! Do you hear that? It's striking two! You'd better hurry to school!"

Already the first gales of spring were roaring around the house; the hour was approaching.

"If I should not survive," thought Inez, "I wonder if he would then remember me too?"

With fearsome eyes she walked past the door of the room which was waiting her and her future destiny in silence; she took soft steps, as if there were something in there which she was afraid of waking.

And at last a child, a second little girl, had been born to the house. Outside the pale green twigs were tapping on the windows, but inside the young mother lay pale and disfigured; the warm suntan of the cheeks had vanished, but in her eyes burned a fire that was consuming her body. Rudolf sat by the bed and held her slender hand in his.

Now she turned her head with an effort towards the cradle which stood on the other side of the room under old Annie's care. "Rudolf," she said weakly, "I have one more request!"

"One more, Inez? I shall have many requests to make of you."

She looked at him sadly; only for a second; then her eye sped hastily back to the cradle. "You know," said she, breathing more and more heavily, "there is no portrait of me! You always said it should only be painted by a good master. We can't wait any longer for the master hand. You might send for a photographer, Rudolf; it is a little difficult, but my child won't get to know me any more; it must know what its mother looked like."

"Wait just a little while," said he, trying to put a note of courage into his voice. "It would excite you too much just now; wait until your cheeks fill out again!"

She passed both hands over her black hair, which lay long and glossy on the coverlet, while she cast an almost wild glance about the room.

"A mirror!" she said, as she raised herself up out of the pillows. "Bring me a mirror!"

He wanted to prevent it, but the old woman had already fetched a hand mirror and laid it on the bed. The sick woman seized it hastily, but as she looked into it, a vivid terror was depicted in her features; she took a cloth and wiped at the glass, but that wrought no change; ever stranger grew the ailing countenance that stared out at her.

"Who is that?" she suddenly shrieked. "That is not I! O, my God! No picture, no shadow for my child!"

She dropped the mirror and covered her face with her emaciated hands.

The sound of weeping reached her ears. It was not her child, which lay asleep in its cradle, unaware; Aggie had stolen in unobserved; she stood in the middle of the room and looked with tragic eyes at her stepmother, while she sobbed and bit her lips.

Inez had perceived her. "You are crying, Aggie?" she asked.

But the child did not answer.

"Why are you crying, Aggie?" she repeated with vehemence.

The features of the child darkened still more. "For my mother!" came the words almost defiantly from her little mouth.

The stepmother was startled for a moment, but then she stretched out her arms, and as the child, as if against her will, had come closer, she drew it passionately to her breast. "O Aggie, don't forget your mother!"

Then two little arms closed around her neck, and she alone understood the whisper, "My dear, sweet Mama!"

"Am I your dear Mama, Aggie?"

Aggie did not answer; she merely nodded hard at the pillows.

"Well then, Aggie," said she in a blissful and confiding whisper, "don't forget me either! O, I don't want to be forgotten!"

Rudolf had watched these proceedings without stirring, not daring to disturb them; half in mortal fear, half in secret rejoicing, but fear kept the upper hand. Inez had sunk back among her pillows; she spoke no more; she slept suddenly.

Aggie, who had softly withdrawn from the bed, knelt by her little sister's cradle; full of admiration she studied the tiny hand that stuck up out of the cushions, and when the little red face puckered itself up and the tiny helpless human sound came from it, her eyes shone with delight. Rudolf, who had quietly come forwards, laid his hand in a caress on her head; she turned around and kissed her father's other hand; then she looked down at her sister again.

The hours advanced. Outside the noonday light shone, and the curtains at the windows were drawn more tightly. He had been sitting this long time beside the bed of his beloved wife, in brooding expectation; thoughts and images came and went; he did not look at them, but let them come and go. On a former occasion it had been as it was now; an uncanny feeling came over him; he felt as if he were living a second life. Again he saw the black tree of death rise up and cover his whole house with its dark branches. Anxiously he looked towards Inez, but she was slumbering quietly; her breast rose in tranquil breathing. Under the window among the blossoming lilacs a little bird sang incessantly; he did not hear it; he was at pains to drive away the deceptive hopes that were now trying to spin their web about him.

In the afternoon the physician came; he bent down over the sleeper and took her hand, which was covered with a warm moisture. Rudolf looked intently into the face of his friend, whose features took on an expression of surprise.

"Do not spare me!" he said. "Let me know all!"

But the doctor pressed his hand.

"Saved!" That was the only word he could recall. All at once he heard the song of the bird; life in its entirety came flooding back. "Saved!" And he had already given her up, her too, as lost into the vast night; he had thought that the violent agitation of the morning must destroy her, but not so:

"It brought her new life,
It snatched her from drowning!"

Into these words of the poet he compressed all his happiness; like music they went on ringing in his ears.

And still the patient went on sleeping; still he sat at her bed and waited. Only the night lamp was now giving light in the silent room; from the garden outside there now came, instead of birdsongs, the murmur of the night wind; sometimes it swelled like the tones of a harp and then sped by; the young twigs tapped softly on the windows.

"Inez!" he whispered. "Inez!" He could not desist from uttering her name.

Then she opened her eyes and let them rest on him strong and long, as if her soul must climb up from the depths of sleep before it could reach him.

"You, Rudolf?" she said at last. "And I have waked up once more?"

He looked at her and could not satiate himself with the sight of her. "Inez," he said, his voice sounded almost humble, "I have been sitting here for hours, bearing this happiness on my head like a burden; help me carry it, Inez!"

"Rudolf!" She had raised herself up with a vigorous movement.

"You will live, Inez!"

"Who said so?"

"My friend, the doctor; I know he was not deceived."

"Live! O good God! Live! For my child, for you!" It was as if a recollection suddenly came to her; she clasped her husband's neck with her hands and pressed his ear to her mouth. "And for your, no, our Aggie!" she whispered. Then she released his neck, and seizing both his hands, she spoke to him gently and lovingly. "I feel so unburdened!" she said. "Now I have no idea why everything was so hard up to now!" And then, nodding at him, "You shall see, Rudolf; now the good time is coming! But," and she lifted her head and brought her eyes quite close to his, "I must have a share in your past, you must tell me the whole story of your happiness! And, Rudolf, her sweet picture shall hang in the room that belongs to us both; she must be present when you tell me."

He looked at her like one blessed.

"Yes, Inez; she shall be present!"

"And Aggie! I will tell her things about her mother that I have heard from you – things suited to her age, Rudolf, only such things…"

He could only nod silently.

"Where is Aggie?" she then enquired. "I should just like to kiss her good night!"

"She is sleeping, Inez," he said, gently stroking her forehead with his hand. "You know it is midnight!"

"Midnight! Then you must sleep now, too! But I – don't laugh at me, Rudolf – I am hungry; I must eat something! And then, after that, put the cradle beside my bed; quite close, Rudolf! Then I too will sleep some more; I feel that; positively, you can go away without concern."

But he remained.

"First I must have a pleasure!" he said.

"A pleasure?"

"Yes, Inez, a wholly new one; I want to watch you eat!"

"O you!"

And when he had had this satisfaction too, he and the nurse carried the cradle over to her bed.

"And now good night! I feel as if I were to sleep into our wedding day again."

But she pointed to the child with a happy smile.

And soon all was still. But it was not the black tree of death that spread its branches over the roof of the house; from distant fields of golden grain the red poppies of sleep were softly nodding. A rich harvest was still in prospect. And again it was the time of roses. On the broad path of the big garden stood a merry vehicle. Nero had clearly been promoted; for he was now harnessed not to a doll carriage but to a real baby carriage and he patiently held still while Aggie tightened the last buckle on his huge head. Old Annie was bending down to the sunshade of the little carriage and pulling at the cushions in which the little daughter of the house, still unnamed, lay with big eyes open, but already Aggie was crying, "Get up, old Nero!" and at a dignified pace the little caravan set itself in motion for its daily ride.

Rudolf and Inez, who clung to his arm, more beautiful than ever, had looked on smiling; now they took their own course; they struck off to one side through the shrubs along the garden wall, and soon they were standing before the locked gate. The bushes did not hang down as formerly; a trellis had been built up under them, so that one got to the gate as through a shady arbored walk. For a moment they listened to the polyphonic bird-choir, having its own way in the undisturbed solitude beyond. But then, compelled by Inez's vigorous little hands, the key turned, and the bolt sprang back with a creaking noise. Inside they heard the birds swoop upward, and then all was still. The gate stood open by a hand's breadth, but on the inside it was held by a network of blossoming vines; Inez put forth all her strength, and there was a crackle and rustle behind it, but the door was caught.

"You'll have to do it!" she said at last, looking up exhausted but smiling at her husband.

The masculine hand forced the entrance; then Rudolf carefully laid the torn vines back on either side.

Before them the gravel path now shimmered in the full sunlight, but softly, as if it were still that moonlit night, they walked around on it between the dark-green conifers, past the cabbage roses, whose hundreds of blooms gleamed out from the rampant bushes, and under the tumble-down rush roof at the end of the path, in front of which the clematis had now spun its web all over the garden chair. Inside the hut, as in the preceding summer, the swallow had built her nest; it flew in and out over their heads without fear.

What did they say to each other? For Inez too this was now holy ground. At times they were silent, merely listening to the hum of the insects which were playing outside in the scented air. Years ago Rudolf had heard the same sounds; it had always been like that. People died; were these little music-makers eternal?

"Rudolf, I have discovered something!" Inez resumed. "Just take the first letter of my name and put it at the end! Then what do you get?"

"Nesi!"* he said with a smile. "That is a wonderful coincidence."

"You see!" she continued, "so Aggie really has my name. So isn't it reasonable that my child should get her mother's name? Marie! That sounds so good and gentle; you know it's not unimportant, the name a child hears itself called!"

He was silent for a moment.

"Let us not play with these things!" he said then, looking fondly into her eyes. "No, Inez; not even with the face of my dear little child shall her portrait be painted over for me. Not Marie, and not Inez – as your mother wished – shall the child be named! Inez too exists for me but once in all the world, and never again." And after a while he added, "Will you now say that you have an obstinate husband?"

"No, Rudolf; only this, that you are Aggie's true father!"

"And you, Inez?"

"Just have patience; I shall become your true wife! But—"

"Is there still a 'but'?"

"Not a bad one, Rudolf! But – when once time is over – for someday the end will come – when we are all in that place that you don't believe in, but that you perhaps hope for – the place to which she has preceded us; then" – and she raised herself up to him and put both hands about his neck – "don't push me away, Rudolf! Don't attempt it; I will never give you up!"

He enclosed her firmly in his arms and said, "Let us do what is at hand; that is the best thing a person can teach himself and others."

"And what is that?" she asked.

"Live, Inez; as beautifully and as long as we can!"

Now they heard child-voices from the gate; little sounds that were not yet words, but that penetrate to the heart, and a high-pitched "Git ap!" and "Whoa!" in Aggie's powerful voice. And in the tow of faithful Nero, guarded by the old serving woman, the merry future of the house made its entrance into the garden of the past.

Curator Carsten

Translated by Frieda M. Voigt

H IS REAL NAME was Carsten Carstens,* and he was the son of a humble citizen, from whom he had inherited a home built by his grandfather. It was in the alley by the harbour and included a small business in woollen goods and such wearing apparel as was customarily used by the seamen of the surrounding islands on their voyages. Since however he was of a somewhat brooding disposition and had, like many a North Friesian, an innate bent towards studying, he had occupied himself since earliest childhood with all sorts of books and writings, thus gradually gaining the reputation among his fellows of a man from whom one could procure reliable counsel in doubtful cases. If as a result of his uncommon reading, as could easily happen, his thoughts strayed off onto a path where his neighbours could not follow him, he encouraged no one to do so; consequently he escaped arousing the suspicions of anyone. So he had become the curator of a number of widows and spinsters, whom the laws of that period still required to get such assistance in all legal matters.

Since it was not his own profit, when he arranged the affairs of others, but the interest he took in the work itself which was uppermost, he differed essentially from other persons who were wont to carry out similar duties, and soon the dying knew of no better man to serve as legal guardian of their children, and the courts of no better executor in bankruptcy or inheritance cases, than Carsten Carstens of the Alley, who under the name of "Curator Carsten" was now universally known as a man of impregnable honour.

In view of the many trusteeships which claimed his time, his small business, to be sure, declined into a side line and was managed almost entirely by an unmarried sister who had remained with him in their parental home.

For the rest, Carsten was a man of few words and of quick decisions, and whenever he encountered a base motive he was inexorable, even at his own expense. Once a so-called "ox-grazer", who for years had leased a piece of marshland from him at what was then considered a low rent, solemnly declared that he could not afford that price the next year. Later, when this produced no result, he agreed to renew the lease at the old price after all, and when this offer was likewise rejected, he even raised the rent himself. Carsten however told him that he was far from wishing his land to be the cause of reckless damage, and thereupon he leased the property at the original price to another citizen who had previously approached him about the matter.

And yet there had been a period in his life when men shook their heads over him. Not that he had been remiss in any of the affairs entrusted to him; it was because it seemed that he was becoming unreliable in the regulation of his own affairs. But Death, taking advantage as he often does of a certain occasion, had again brought everything back to normal after a few years.

It was during the blockade of the continent by Napoleon, in the "blockade time", when the little port town filled up with Danish officers and French seamen as well as with many types of foreign speculators, that one of the latter was found hanging in the attic of his warehouse. That this was suicide could not be doubted, for the affairs of the deceased, after several losses in quick succession, had suffered ruin; the only real asset of his estate was said to be his daughter, pretty Juliana. Up to this time, however, many viewers but no buyers had turned up.

The very next morning Carsten received the young girl's request to take charge of the regulation of her affairs, but he refused the request, saying only, "I want to have no dealings with those people." However, when the old longshoreman who had brought the message returned in the afternoon and said, "Don't be so hard, Carstens; there's nobody left but the girl, and she's crying that she'll have to lay hands on herself," he quickly got up, took his cane, and followed the messenger into the house of the dead.

In the middle of the room into which the man led him stood the open coffin with the corpse in it; next to it, on a low stool with her knees drawn up, sat a beautiful girl, half-dressed. She held a tortoise-shell comb in her hand and was drawing it through her thick golden-blonde hair, which hung down her back unbraided. Her eyes were red and her lips trembling with violent weeping; it was hard to say whether because of perplexity or grief at her father's death.

When Carsten advanced towards her she rose and received him with reproaches: "You won't help me?" she cried, "and I don't understand anything about anything. What am I to do? My father had lots of money, but probably there's none left. There he lies now; do you want me to lie there like that too?"

She sat down on her stool again, and Carsten looked at her almost in astonishment. "You see, Mademoiselle," he said then, "I'm here to help you. Won't you entrust your father's books to me?"

"Books? I know of none, but I'll look around." She went into an adjoining room and soon returned with a bunch of keys. "Here," she said, laying them on the table before Carsten, "you're said to be a good man; do whatever you like; I won't bother about anything now."

Carsten saw with surprise how attractive she was as she spoke these frivolous words; for a sigh of relief passed through her whole body, and a smile like sudden sunshine crossed her pretty face.

And just as she had said, so it turned out: Carsten worked, and she never bothered about anything. He could never make out how she spent her time. But her full red lips laughed again, and her black mourning outfit turned into a seductive costume. Once, on hearing her sigh, he asked whether she had some sorrow; if so, she should tell him.

She looked at him with a faint smile. "Oh, Mr Carstens," she said, sighing again, "it is so boring not to be allowed to dance in these black clothes." Then like a frolicsome child she asked him whether he didn't think she might soon change her dress just once, at least for one evening; her father had always permitted her to dance, and now he'd been buried for a long time.

When Carsten nevertheless said no, she went off pouting. She had long since noticed that this was her best way of punishing him for his moral austerity. For while he had succeeded in resolving the financial confusion of the dead man's affairs to the point at least where debit and credit seemed to balance, he had himself got into a different confusion: the laughing eyes of pretty Juliana had infatuated the forty-year-old man. What might otherwise have caused him to hesitate appeared to him at this time, when the even course of civic life was completely suppressed, much less hazardous, and on the other hand the girl, unaccustomed to work as she was, preferred a secure refuge to the hardships which otherwise awaited her. So, despite sister Brigitta's head-shaking, a marriage ceremony soon took place between these two dissimilar people. The sister, to be sure, who was now all the more indispensable in the household, got nothing from the marriage but a double load of work, but the sudden possession of so much youth and beauty, to which he believed neither his person nor his age entitled him, filled her brother with an exuberant feeling of gratitude, which made him only too indulgent to the wishes of his young wife. So it came about that the usually quiet man was soon to be seen at all the festivities whereby the foreign officers endeavoured to reduce the excess of their leisure hours. This was a sociability not only beyond his station and his means, but also one into which he was drawn solely on his wife's account, while he himself played an unheeded and awkward role.

However, Juliana died in her first childbirth. "How happy I'll be when I can dance again!" she had exclaimed repeatedly during her pregnancy, but she was never to dance again, and thus Carsten was rid of that danger. Of happiness also, to be sure; for even though she had hardly belonged to him, as she perhaps could not really belong to anyone, and no matter how one might chide her, yet it had been she who had let the light of her beauty shine into his workaday life; a strange butterfly which had flown across his garden and which his eyes continued to follow long after it had disappeared from his sight. Otherwise Carsten again became, in fact to a greater degree than before, the sensible and calmly deliberating man.

The boy whom the deceased had left him, and who soon proved to be the physical, and in time also the mental heir of his beautiful mother, was brought up with a strictness which Carsten had to wrest from his own heart. The good-natured yet easily-tempted darling was spared no merited punishment; only when the child's beautiful eyes, as invariably happened in such cases, looked up at him with a kind of helpless terror, the father had to restrain himself forcibly from immediately taking the boy with passionate tenderness back into his arms.

More than twenty years had passed since Juliana's death. Heinrich – so he had been baptized after his paternal grandfather – had gone to school and from school into mercantile apprenticeship, but nothing in his innate character had noticeably changed. His cleverness made him adapt himself easily to any situation, but he too, like his mother before him, looked charming when he threw back his head with the light-brown curls and laughingly called to his comrades, "It must be possible! We won't bother about a thing!" And indeed this was the only matter as to which he conscientiously kept his word: he did not bother about anything, or at least only about things which he would have done better not to bother about. His aunt Brigitta often wept over him, and Carsten too felt something lay itself beside him on the pillow of his alcove bed, something which, he knew not how, kept sleep away; when he sat up and reflected, he would see his boy before him, and it seemed to him as if he feared to see him grow up.

But Heinrich did not remain the only child of the house. A distant relative, bound to Carsten by mutual affection, died suddenly, leaving an eight-year-old daughter. Since the child had lost its mother at birth, Carsten fulfilled the dying man's wish by not only becoming little Anna's guardian, but also taking her into his home and caring for her completely. He proved his loyalty to his deceased relative however in a very special act: by furnishing credit and advancing loans for the daughter, not without risk to him in those days, he acquired a small country estate for her, which later under better economic conditions could be sold at a sizable profit.

Anna had taken after a different kind of mother than Heinrich, her senior by one year. In spite of the best intentions he never succeeded in considering his own, any more than his closest kinfolks' weal or woe in any of his doings; while Anna on the other hand – how often Aunt Brigitta reached into her pocket and gave her a small coin as indemnity, accompanying her smacking kiss with the remark, "You foolish girl, you've completely forgotten to think of yourself again!" But to her brother, when she could get hold of him, she would say at such times, "Cousin Martin certainly meant well by us; he left us his blessing!"

Together with her kind-heartedness the girl also had a cheerfully reliable nature, and when Carsten at times anxiously enquired of Brigitta about Heinrich's whereabouts and received the answer, "He's with Anna; she's sewing sails for his boats," or, "She just came to get him – she wants him to help her mend the cherry-tree nets," then he would nod and sit down to his work with an easy mind.

At the time when we continue this story, on a morning in late summer, Anna had just come of age and as a full-grown blonde young girl was standing with her grey-haired guardian before the mayor in the city hall, where the necessary legal steps were to be taken.

"Uncle," she had said before entering the courtroom, "I'm afraid."

"You are, child? That's not like you."

"I know, Uncle, but this elegant vestibule!"

The scrawny old man, who felt quite at home there, had smiled at the eager girlish face which was looking up at him with flushed cheeks, and then pushed open the door to the courtroom.

But the mayor was a jovial gentleman. "My dear child," he said, surveying her with pleasure, "you know of course that you will again become a minor, but only when you let a gold ring be slipped on your finger. May your life then be entrusted to just as faithful a hand."

He glanced at Carsten with a warm expression. But when the girl heard the judge praise her guardian thus, although a faint flush overspread her pretty face, all her embarrassment vanished. Calmly she had the record of her property brought before her, and, as was requested of her, read everything through carefully and intelligently. Then almost uneasily she said, "Eight thousand talers! No, Uncle, that won't do!"

"What won't do, child?" asked Carsten.

"This paper, Uncle – about all those talers" – and she stood up before him in all her youthful dignity – "What am I to do with them? You haven't taught me that. No, Your Honour, pardon me, but I cannot come of age today."

The two old men laughed and said it was no use: she was of age and would have to remain so. But Carsten added, "Don't worry, Anna; I'll be your curator, just ask the Mayor to appoint me as such."

"Curator, Uncle? I know that's what people call you."

"Yes, child, but now it's like this: you continue to care for my old sister's and my own body and soul, and I'll go on helping you bear the burden of these awful talers. I think that's the right way to do it."

"Amen," said the old mayor; then the acknowledgment of the proper legal management of her fortune was signed by Anna in her neat hand.

While she and Carsten were taking their leave, the mayor, as if seeking relief from official business, glanced out of the window to the street.

"Oh my!" he cried, "here comes Mr Jaspers, the broker! What does that bearer of bad news have to dish out to me now?"

Carsten smiled and involuntarily took his foster daughter by the hand. As the two of them began to descend the wide stairs to the first floor, a short, oldish man in a worn brown suit came up them. Reaching the landing, he leant panting on his light cane and stared up at Carsten and Anna out of little grey eyes, lifting his high top hat off his fox-red wig several times.

Carsten was going to pass with a brief "Good morning," but the other extended his cane in front of the two. "Oho, my friend!" It was a truly old-womanish voice that crowed out of the little wrinkled face. "You don't get by me like that!"

"The Mayor is waiting for you," said Carsten, and pushed the cane aside.

"The Mayor?" Mr Jaspers laughed quite gleefully. "Let him wait. This time I was looking for you, my friend; I knew that you would be around here somewhere."

"For me, Jaspers?" repeated Carsten, and in his voice was an uncertainty which was not usual with him. As had long been the case when something unexpected was made known to him, the thought of his Heinrich had shot through his head. The latter was at present employed by a local Senator, but the stern old man, with whom Carsten himself had served an apprenticeship under his father, had thus far shown himself to be satisfied with the young lad and had only once said a sharp word about him. Only yesterday, on Sunday, Heinrich had returned from a business trip for his employer. No, no; Mr Jaspers could not have anything to tell about Heinrich.

Mr Jaspers had meanwhile been looking up with wide-open mouth to the much taller Carsten and observed with evident pleasure his changing facial expression. "Ha, my friend," he cried now, and his voice had a ring of inviting cheerfulness. "You know, things could always be even worse, and even if you lose your head, there's always a stump left."

"What do you want of me, Jaspers?" Carsten asked gloomily. "Out with it here and now, then you'll be rid of the load."

But Mr Jaspers tugged at his coat-tail to bring his ear down within reach. "These are no matters to be mentioned here in the city hall." Then he added, turning to the girl, "Surely Mademoiselle Anna can find her way home alone." And once more tipping his top hat with his nervous hand that seemed always to be clutching at something, he energetically stamped down the stairs again.

When they had stepped out of the building, he pointed with his cane to a side street, at the corner of which was his home. Anna glanced enquiringly at her guardian, but he silently motioned her away and followed as if under a paralysing spell the "civic bearer of bad news", who now eagerly pushed up the street with him.

In the little yard behind Carsten's house there stood not only the cherry tree for which the children had once mended net coverings, but also on the long side of the bleaching lawn an enormous pear tree, which was the joy of the neighbourhood children and at the same time a kind of family shrine. It had been planted by the grandfather of the present owner and later grafted by the father with three kinds of pear which were most popular in the city, and these, now grown into fully developed boughs, bore, each in its special season, an abundance of succulent fruits. To be sure, nothing that could be reached with the well-pole found its way into the house; otherwise the children couldn't have been allowed such ready access to Mistress Anna. As it was, however, whenever the neighbours to the west heard hearty girlish laughter, they knew that Anna was busy at the tree and that the young fry were romping and scuffling on the grass over the pears she knocked down.

Now too, as Anna on her return from the city hall was about to enter the house, she had picked up such a chubby neighbourhood urchin. In the hall, a cool room paved with stone slabs at the back of the vestibule, she took off hat and scarf, and holding the child astride on her outstretched arms she stepped through the door leading to the yard and into the shade of the great tree.

"You see, darling," she said, "up there lies the cat – she'd like to have that nice yellow pear too! But wait a minute, I'll get the pole."

But as she turned towards the well which lay behind the yard door, she cried out and let the child drop, almost with a thud. On the rotten wooden coping, the repair of which had only been delayed by an accident, sat her youthful comrade, her playmate, his feet hanging over the opening, his head bent forwards as if about to plunge into it.

But in the next instant she was there too, had embraced him with both arms from behind and pulled him back, so that the rotten boards collapsed under him with a crash. She had fallen to her knees, while the pale, almost girlishly pretty head of the young man still rested on her breast.

He did not move; it seemed as if he had submitted apathetically to everything that was happening to him. Even when the girl finally jumped up, he remained, without looking at her, lying among the broken boards with propped up head. She however looked at him almost in anger, and tears leapt into her blue eyes.

"What ails you, Heinrich? Why did you frighten me so? Why aren't you at the Senator's office?"

Now he stroked his silken-soft hair back from his forehead and looked at her wearily. "I'm not going back to the Senator's," he said.

"Not back to the Senator's?"

"No; for I have only two roads left: either here into the well or to the bailiff and prison."

"What nonsense are you saying? Get up, Heinrich! Have you gone mad?"

He arose obediently and let her lead him to the little bench under the pear tree. But there was the child, who had been watching everything with astonished eyes. "Poor thing," said Anna, "you haven't got a pear yet. Here, buy yourself a little cake!" And as the child ran off with the coin, the girl again stood before the young man.

"Now speak up!" she said, while she pinned up her heavy blonde braid, which had fallen down her back. "Speak quickly, before father gets back."

Her breathing quickened as she waited for an answer, but he was silent and stared down at the ground.

"You came back from Flensburg Saturday!" she said then. "You were to collect money for the Senator."

He nodded without looking up.

"Just tell me! I can imagine: you were careless again; you left the money lying about, in the hotel or somewhere. And now it's gone!"

"Yes, it's gone," he said.

"But maybe we can get it back. Why don't you speak? Tell me about it!"

"No, Anna – it's not lost the way you think. We were gay; we gambled—"

"Gambled away, Heinrich? Gambled away?" Tears gushed from her eyes, and she threw herself on his breast, both arms clasped about his neck.

81

Up in the treetop a light wind rustled in the leaves; otherwise there was no sound but an occasional deep sob from the girl, in whom all the activity she had displayed just before seemed broken now.

But the young man himself tried gently to push her from him; the lovely burden which compassion had thrown on his breast seemed to be crushing him.

"Don't cry like that," he said, "I can't stand it."

There was no need for this admonition; Anna had already jumped up and was trying quickly to wipe away her tears. "Heinrich," she cried, "it is terrible that you did it, but I have money, I'll help you!"

"You, Anna?"

"Yes, I! I just came of age. Tell me how much you have to deliver to the Senator."

"It's a lot," he said hesitantly.

"How much? Tell me quickly!" He named a considerable amount. "Not more? Thank God! But…" And she faltered, as if a new obstacle had loomed up before her. "You should have been at the office today. What will you tell the Senator when he asks?"

Heinrich shook his soft curls from his brow, and already the old expression of carefree light-heartedness passed over his face. "The Senator, Anna? Oh, he won't ask, and if he does – let me take care of that."

She gazed at him earnestly. "See, now we'll have to begin lying!"

"Only I, Anna, and I promise you, no more than necessary. And the money—"

"Yes, the money!"

"I'll pay you interest, Anna, I'll write you a promissory note – you shall not lose anything on my account."

"Stop talking nonsense, Heinrich. Stay here in the garden; when your father gets home, I'll ask him for the money."

He wanted to reply, but she had already gone back into the house. She crept cautiously past the kitchen, where Aunt Brigitta was taking her place at the stove today, and then she ran up into her room, first of all to wash away all traces of weeping from her eyes.

The furniture and equipment of the narrow living room, whose bay windows faced the harbour, were of not much more recent date than the old pear tree. In the alcove bed there deep inside the bay, whose glass doors were closed in the daytime, the parents of the owner had lain down for their nightly and, in succession, also for their eternal sleep; at that time, as well as now, there stood in the west corner of the bay the leather-covered armchair in which the old captains after completing their purchases were wont to unravel their yarns before the master of the house as he sat facing them. The things had remained the same; only quite unnoticeably other people had been substituted, and while such reports of foreign countries had once supplied the late father Carstens merely with material for pleasant retelling, they often aroused in the son a chain of thoughts for the elaboration of which he was thrown on his own resources.

The table which stood at the bay windows between a straight chair and the leather armchair had also retained its own position; only the exotic shells, which now served on the table as paperweights for all kinds of writings, had formerly adorned the cash box standing near by. In their stead the present owner had had a little bookcase built, in which besides a few mathematical works and the chronicles of the city and its environs there were also books like Lessing's *Nathan** and Hippel's *Careers in an Ascending Line.**

No sofa had been brought into the room, nor would there have been room for one. On the other hand, a rather stately ancestral portrait was not lacking, by the contemplation of which the humble citizen Carsten, even if not in the French formulation of "noblesse oblige", used to strengthen his wavering spirit in difficult hours.

This was to be sure no bright-coloured oil painting, but quite on the contrary only an enormous silhouette framed in glass moulding painted brown, which hung on the west wall nearest the bay, so that from his work table the owner could let his eyes rest on it. His father, about whom admittedly not much more can be said than that he was a simple and austere man, had had it done, soon after the death of his wife, by a transient artist. It represented an evening stroll of the now half-orphaned family. The father himself took the lead, a lean figure like the son now living, wearing a three-cornered hat and a roquelaure, and holding the arm of a bent old lady, the mother of the deceased; then came a tall tree of undetermined species, but clearly suggesting late autumn, for its branches were almost bare, and here and there under the glass of the picture clung little black shreds which with some imagination might be identified as fallen leaves. Then followed a boy of about four years, gaily riding a hobby-horse and brandishing a whip. The family group was completed by a girl like a beanpole and another boy about ten years old, with a cap as round as a dinner plate, both of whom, as it seemed, lost in admiration of the lively hobby-horseman, had no eyes for the charm of the evening landscape. And yet this was just the right hour for it, as was ingeniously worked out in the picture; for while in the foreground trees and people were cut out of coal-black paper, to the rear were the lines of a gently elevated plain, with a suggestion of evening distance, formed first of dark and then of light-grey blotting paper. The rest however had been completed by painting; beyond the reach of the eye a mildly gleaming afterglow suffused the whole horizon, making the shadows of all the strollers all the more sharply outlined; higher up, in brownish-purple twilight, night was descending.

Soon after the completion of the picture the jolly little rider had been snatched away by smallpox, and only his little hobbyhorse had for a long time stood in the case of the wall clock, which, facing the picture, now as then tried to measure the flight of time with its even tick-tock. Of the five evening strollers only the two older siblings were still living, under the same roof as at that time, and, even during the brief marriage of the brother, unseparated. Sometimes, in a quiet evening hour or when sorrow overcame them, they had found themselves – they themselves hardly knew how – hand in hand before the picture, reviving from memory the nature and the deeds of their parents. "There are the rest of us, still together," the father had said when he hung the picture on the same nail which supported it now. "Your mother is no longer here, but instead we have the afterglow in the sky." And then after a while, having turned his face away from the children and given the nail a couple of heavy blows with the hammer, "A light still remains on earth from the dead, too, and those left behind should not forget that they stand in this light, so that they may keep their hands and faces clean."

Aunt Brigitta, who as an old maid was somewhat given to sighing, and with complete unselfishness loved to build air castles in the past, after such reminiscing used to point to the silhouette of the little hobbyhorse rider and add, "Ah, Carsten, if only our brother Peter were still alive! Don't you think too that he was the smartest of us three children?" And the conversation between brother and sister might then take the following course.

"What do you mean, Brigitta?" the brother would reply. "He was only in his fifth year when he died."

"Yes, unfortunately he did die so young, Carsten, but you remember how our big yellow-speckled hen always laid her eggs behind the ash pile. He was only four years old, but he was already smarter than the hen; he would let her lay her eggs, and then one fine morning he would bring me a whole apron-full into the kitchen. Ah, Carsten, you know the Senator's father was his godfather; he surely would have gone to the Latin school and not, like you, only learnt his letters and numbers."

And the living brother was always glad to acknowledge such a preference for the brother who had died so very young.

The room with its old furnishings and its old memories was still empty, although only the row of lindens in front of the house obstructed the rays of the sun, which had now reached its zenith. The white sea sand with which Anna had strewn the floors before her trip to the city hall showed hardly any footprints, and the old wall clock ticked as loudly in the solitude as if it wanted to call its master to his customary work. Now finally the doorbell rang and Anna, sitting expectantly up in her room, heard the steps of her foster father, who immediately disappeared downstairs into the living room. After a while, she then braced herself to a quick decision, patted her eyes a few more times with a moist cloth, and went down to the first floor.

As she entered the living room she saw her foster father standing with his hat and his cane still in his hand, almost as if he must consider what to do now within his own four walls. Fear gripped the girl; it seemed to her as if he had suddenly become unspeakably old. She would have liked to slip away again unnoticed, but she had no time to lose.

"Uncle!" she said softly.

The sound of her voice almost startled him, but when he saw the girl standing before him, a friendly light came into his eyes. "What do you want of me, my child?" he asked gently.

"Uncle!" Only hesitantly did she utter it. "I am of age now; I would like to have some of my money now; I have urgent need of it."

"So soon, Anna? That's quick indeed."

"Not much, Uncle; I mean, I have so much more; only about a hundred talers."

She was silent, and the old man looked down at her a while without speaking. "And what would you want to do with all that money?" he then asked.

An imploring glance from her eyes found him; she murmured something which he did not understand.

He took her hand. "Just say it out loud, my child."

"I didn't want it for myself," she replied falteringly.

"Not for yourself, for whom else then?"

Like a pleading child she raised her hands towards him. "Don't make me say it, Uncle! Oh, but I must, I must have it!"

"And not for yourself, Anna?" As if suddenly understanding, he let his eyes rest on her. "If you wanted it for Heinrich – then both of us have already come too late."

"Oh no, Uncle! No!" And she flung her arms about the old man's neck.

"Yes, child, it's true. What else do you think Mr Jaspers had to tell me? The Senator was informed of everything yesterday."

"But if Heinrich takes the money to him now?"

"I wanted to take it to him myself, but he wanted neither my money nor my son. And as far as the latter is concerned – I could not say anything to the contrary."

"Oh, Uncle, what will happen to him?"

"To him, Anna? He will leave that honourable house in disgrace."

As she raised in fright her pure countenance towards her foster father, such an expression of suffering met her gaze as she had never before seen on any human face. "Uncle, Uncle!" she cried. "What crime did *you* commit?" And her maidenly eyes expressed such a maternal pity that the old man let his grey head sink on her shoulder.

Then however straightening up and laying his hand on her blonde hair he said quietly, "I, Anna, am his father. Now go and call my son to me."

This day, too, passed. After the grievous forenoon came a noon meal and later an evening meal at which the dishes were removed almost as they were placed on the table; between the meals a seemingly endless afternoon, during which Heinrich, compelled by the superior will of his father, once more had to return to the Senator and was dismissed by him. This day, too, had finally passed and night had come. Only the master of the house was still pacing to and fro in the downstairs room; occasionally he stopped in front of the picture with the family shadows, but soon passed his hand across his brow and continued his unquiet wandering. Anna had also been at the Senator's, in a swift, youthful resolve, but of that he had as little notion as of the fact that the Senator had barely managed to maintain his inexorable stand before her, but had finally done so.

The small shaded lamp which was burning on his work table shone on two letters, one addressed to Kiel, the other to Hamburg; for new ways had to be sought out for Heinrich, away from home.

Carsten had stepped to the window and looked out into the moonlit night; it was so quiet that he could hear the water from the gutters flow into the harbour far below, and now and then a faint flutter in the pennants of the ships off shore. Across the harbour the mole extended out like a shimmering fog bank; how often as a boy he had walked out there hand in hand with his father, to inspect the fen they had acquired at that time.

Carsten slowly turned around; there lay the two letters on his work table; he had a son himself now.

In the depth of the room the glass doors of the alcove had been opened by Anna, as on every other evening, and the turned-back covers of the bed in there seemed to invite Carsten, accustomed as he was to the hours of the solid citizen, to make an end of the overlong day. And so he took his big silver watch from its case and wound it. "Midnight," he said, as he stepped into the alcove. But as he tried to hang the watch on the bed post, in accordance with his habit, the steel chain hooked itself in a gold ring he wore on his little finger, so that the ring was torn off and rolled away on the floor with a faint clink. With almost youthful quickness the old man bent down for it, and when the ring was back in his hand again he stepped back into the room and carefully held it under the lamp shade. His eyes seemed fixed on the woman's name inscribed on the inside, but from his mouth burst a groan, as if he were begging for deliverance.

Just then he heard the steps of the staircase in the hallway creaking. He made a quick motion, as if to place the ring on his finger, when a hand was gently laid on his arm. "Brother Carsten," said his old sister, who had entered the room in her nightgown, "I heard you walking down here; aren't you ever going to try to rest?"

He gazed into her eyes as if reflecting. "There are thoughts, Brigitta, which won't give us rest, which keep forever rising up in our brain, because they are never released."

The old spinster looked at her brother in complete bewilderment. "Oh, Carsten," she said, "I am a stupid old thing! Had only our brother Peter remained alive! Maybe he would be our minister now and would have baptized and confirmed our Heinrich; he would surely have known what to do today, too!"

"Perhaps, Brigitta," gently replied the brother, "and yet perhaps we might not have understood one another completely, but you are alive and are my faithful old sister."

"Yes, yes, Carsten, unfortunately! We two alone are left."

He had taken her hand. "Brigitta," he said quickly, "did you see how pale the boy was when he went up to his room this evening? Never before had he resembled his mother so much; that's how Juliana looked in her last days, when death had already taken all earthly thoughts from her."

"Don't speak of her, brother; that isn't good for you now; she's been at rest a long time."

"A long time, Brigitta – but not here, not here!" And he pressed the hand which was still clasped about the ring against his breast. "It all keeps coming back to me; last Easter Sunday it was just twenty-three years ago."

"Last Easter Sunday? Yes, yes, brother, now I remember it clearly; at that time the two of you were where you never should have been."

"Don't scold now, sister," said Carsten, "you yourself could not turn your eyes from her, as you tied the blue sash around her that day. Now I know of course that it was not for me she pinned up her beautiful hair, and put the satin slippers on her tiny feet; I didn't belong in that company of elegant and exuberant people, where nobody paid any attention to me, least of all my own wife. No, no," he cried, as his sister tried to interrupt him, "Let me say it at last! You see, I did want to play my full part, and I danced with my wife a few times, but she was always snatched from me by the officers. And how differently she danced with those men! Her eyes glowed with pleasure; she passed from hand to hand; I was afraid they would dance my wife to death. But she could not get enough and only laughed when I begged her to spare herself. I couldn't bear it any longer and yet I couldn't change it; that's why I sat down in the side room where the old gentlemen were playing their ombre, and gnawed at my nails and my own thoughts.

"You know, Brigitta, that captain of a French privateer whom the others called the 'handsome devil' – whenever I'd look into the dance hall from time to time, she'd always be dancing with him. When it was almost three o'clock and the dance hall already half-deserted, she stood next to him at the bar, each of them holding a full glass of champagne. I saw how fast she was breathing and how his words, which I could not understand, again and again caused a quick flush to cover her pale face; she herself said nothing, she only stood in silence before him, but as both of them now raised their glasses to their lips, I saw how their eyes melted into each other. I saw all that like a picture, as if it were a hundred miles away from me; then however it suddenly came over me that that beautiful woman belonged to me, that she was my wife, and then I walked up to them and forced her to go home with me."

Carsten hesitated, as if he had reached the limit of his story; his breast heaved laboriously, his lean face was flushed. But he had not yet finished; only now he no longer looked down at his sister, but spoke over her head into space.

"And then when we were in our bedroom, when she did not even deign to look at me, but cast off her belt and bodice as if in anger, and then with a jerk snatched the comb from her hair, so that it was as if a golden flood fell over her hips – it is not always as it should be, sister – for what should have repelled me, I almost believe that it only infatuated me all the more."

His sister gently laid her hand on his arm. "Leave the ghost in its tomb, brother; forget her, she did not belong to us."

He paid no heed. "So," he continued, "I had never seen her before; not in our brief marriage and not during our engagement, either. Yet it was not the beauty that our Lord had given her, it was the evil lust still flashing in her eyes that made her so beautiful. And just as on that evening and in that night the same thing happened many times, through many weeks and months, until only half a year before her death was left – when all those strangers left our city."

"Brother Carsten," said Brigitta again, "haven't you enough new sorrow? If you were weak towards your wife, because you loved her more than was good for you – almost a whole lifetime has passed since then – why do you still torture yourself with it now?"

"Now, Brigitta? Yes, why do I tell you all this now? Was she my wife during the time when her senses reeled with frivolous thoughts that had nothing in common with me? And yet from this marriage that poor boy was born. Do you think," and he bent down towards his sister's ear, "that it makes no difference in what hour, with the consent of an all-wise God, a human life issues forth out of nothingness? I tell you, every human being brings his life ready made into the world with him, and all who have given even a single drop to his blood, back through the centuries, have their share in it."

Outside the clock in the church tower struck one. "Leave it to our dear Lord, brother," said Brigitta, "I don't understand what's going through your head from all your books, I only know that the boy, more's the pity, takes after his mother."

Carsten doubtless felt that he had really been speaking to himself, and that now as always he was alone with himself. "Go to bed and sleep, my good old sister," he said, gently pushing her into the hall. "I'll try it too."

On the bottom stair, where Brigitta had left it, a candle was burning with a long snuff. With firmly closed lips and folded hands she once more looked at her brother; then she nodded at him and went upstairs with the candle.

But Carsten was not thinking of sleep; he had only wanted to be alone again. Once more he took the little ring and held it before him; through the narrow frame he saw, as if deep in the past, the airy vision of the beautiful woman, whom no one on earth besides himself still remembered. A blissful self-oblivion lay on his countenance, but then suddenly a pain quivered across it: she seemed to him to be so completely forsaken down there.

Straightening up, he placed the ring on his finger, and it was done with a solemn fervour, as if he wanted to unite the deceased with him once more, and more tightly than when she was alive; just as she had once been, in her beauty and in her weakness, and with the niggardly love which she had once felt for him. Then he walked to the door and listened for any noise from the hall; hearing that everything remained quiet, he went to the stairway and cautiously made his way to his son's bedroom. He found the young man breathing calmly and fast asleep, although the moon was pouring its full light across the bed, which stood by the window. With the light-brown hair that fell over his temples in silky-soft curls, one could have taken the pretty, pale face of the sleeper for that of a woman.

Carsten had stepped close to the bed; a slight tremor passed through his body. "Juliana!" he said. "Your son! He too will tear my heart to pieces." And he added, "My Lord and God, I am willing to suffer for my child, only don't let him get lost!"

At these words, involuntarily spoken aloud, the sleeper opened his eyes; in slumber, however, his soul may have continued to dream of the terrors of the day just past; for as he suddenly saw in the night the burning eyes of the old man and the trembling arm raised above him, he let out a cry, as if he expected the death blow from his father's hand, but then he beseechingly reached up his arms to him.

And with a cry, as if he could not keep his breast from being rent apart, "My child, my only child!" the father collapsed at the bedside of his offending son.

A friend in Hamburg had made it possible for Carsten to place his son in a small business there. Meanwhile, in spite of the respect which he enjoyed in the little town, this family event was discussed unsparingly enough, though to be sure this also occasioned bringing the memory of poor Juliana not very gently from her tomb. Only Carsten himself learnt nothing about this. One day when he had returned from the home of a friendly citizen in an unusually depressed state, Brigitta asked him with concern, "What is wrong, Carsten? You didn't hear anything bad about our Heinrich, I hope?"

"Bad?" replied her brother. "Oh no, Brigitta; since he left no one has even mentioned his name to me." And with lowered head he went to his work table.

Letters from Heinrich came rarely, and often they demanded money, since he said he could not get along in Hamburg on his meagre salary. In other respects life went on quietly; the old pear tree in the yard had bloomed again, and then at the right time and to the joy of the neighbourhood children had borne its fruit. Nothing special had occurred, unless it were that Anna had refused the marriage proposal of a prosperous young citizen; she was not one of those women who are driven into marriage by their blood; she had not yet wanted to leave her old foster parents.

When however, shortly before Christmas, Carsten notified his son of the sudden death of the Senator, a letter followed in a few days, announcing Heinrich's visit for Christmas Eve. The letter contained no request for money; he had not even asked for travelling expenses.

This was really a message of joy, which was immediately proclaimed in the house. And everyone felt a happy unrest as the holiday approached; the handshakes that Carsten was wont to exchange with his old sister in passing became heartier; once in a while he would catch his busy foster daughter, hold her for a moment by both hands, and gaze tenderly into her cheerful eyes.

Finally the afternoon of 24th December had arrived. An expectant activity had reigned in the house; yet soon everything seemed ready for the reception of the Christ child and the guest. From the work table, which today had been freed of all ledgers and account books, there gleamed on the snow-white damask the tea service with the little gold stars, while next to it the freshly baked Christmas cakes shed their fragrance. On the chest of drawers opposite the door Heinrich's gifts had been spread out by the women: a dozen pairs of stockings of the finest zephyr worsted, on which the provident aunt had knit all year long; beside them, neatly made by Anna's hands, a fancy embroidered satin vest and a green silk purse, through whose meshes shone the gold pieces given by Carsten. Carsten himself was just going into the cellar to bring up from his modest stock two very special bottles, which had been presented to him long ago by a grateful client; today for once there was to be no economizing.

Instead of the master of the house it was Aunt Brigitta who entered, holding two brightly polished candlesticks, on which were placed snow-white Russian candles in paper ruffles of equal whiteness, for the twilight of Christmas Eve had already set in. Outside, the groups of little Christmas beggars were already marching, and their carolling rang out: "From heaven on high I come to you."

When Carsten entered again, the candles were already burning; the room looked quite festive. The old siblings turned their faces towards one another and looked at each other affectionately. "It's almost time, Carsten," said Brigitta, "the mail coach always arrives at about four."

Carsten nodded, and after he had hurriedly planted his bottles behind the warm stove, he reached towards the door peg for his hat.

"Shouldn't I go with you, Uncle?" Anna called to him. "There's nothing more for me to do here."

"No, no, my child; I must do this all alone." With these words he took his bamboo cane from the clock case and went out.

At that time the posting station was far up on Norder Street, but the air was completely calm, and a light frosty snow was falling evenly. Carsten walked on vigorously without glancing to right or left, but when he had almost reached his destination, he suddenly heard someone call out, "Ho there, my friend, take me along!" And Mr Jasper's form, not to be mistaken even in the darkness, advanced towards him from a side street, gaily waving a handkerchief. "I can see," he said, "you want to call for your Heinrich at the station. All I've heard is that he's turned out to be quite a fellow, the young rascal."

"But," said Carsten, lengthening his stride, which the other, swinging both arms, strove to match, "I thought, Jaspers, that there was no one you had to look for."

"No, Carsten, thank Heavens. No, no one. But, the deuce, you don't have to run so! One must see what guests are coming for the sweet festival."

They had arrived at a corner near the post station, where a number of people had already gathered to await the arrival of the mail coach, when Mr Jaspers was hailed by a passing court clerk.

"Don't you hear, Jaspers! That man wants to talk with you," said Carsten, who had just heard the rumbling of a heavy wagon from down the street.

But the other man stood like a stone wall. "Oh, Heaven forbid, Carsten! Let that poltroon go his way. I'll stay with you, my friend; who knows what may still happen? You surely know the story of the Flensburg divinity student who was going to lift his sweetheart out of the coach, only to have a black Negro boy land on him."

"I know all your stories, Jaspers," replied Carsten impatiently, "but if you really want to know the truth, I wish to receive my son alone; I don't need you along!"

Mr Jasper's imperturbable answer was drowned out by the cracking of a whip and the blare of a post horn, and immediately thereafter the clumsy wagon rolled before the door of the post building, into the pale beam which the lantern over the door cast upon the street with its light coating of snow. Then the postilion jumped down from the box, the coach door was pulled open by the head ostler, and the people pushed forwards to see the passengers alight.

Carsten had remained standing back in the shadow of the wall. As he was of tall build, he could clearly enough recognize the forms muffled up in coats and furs, which now stepped one by one out of the body of the coach onto the street.

"No one else inside?" called the ostler.

"No, no!" was heard from several directions, and the coach door was slammed shut.

Carsten grasped the crook of his cane and leant on it; his Heinrich had not come. As if absentmindedly he looked at the steaming horses, which were scraping the pavement and shaking their brass harness till their hangings jingled. At last he was just about to walk away when he noticed that he was not the only disappointed person there. A young girl had approached the postilion, who was throwing blankets over his animals, and she seemed to be pressing him with excited questions. "Yes, yes, Miss," he heard the man answer, "it may still be possible; an extra coach is still to come."

"An extra coach!" Carsten repeated the words involuntarily; a deep sigh of relief escaped his breast. He was acquainted with the postilion; he could have asked him, "Is my Heinrich in that one?" But he was not able to move from the spot; with closed lips he stood there and soon saw the coach drive off, looking at the empty tracks visible in the snow, upon which new snow sank down softly and steadily and soon covered them.

It had grown quiet all around him; even Mr Jaspers seemed to have disappeared; the girl had silently placed herself next to him, her arms wrapped in her shawl. Occasionally a doorbell rang, then children's voices sang, "From heaven on high I come to you." The little Christmas carollers with their comforting song of annunciation were still going about from house to house.

Finally something came up the street again, closer and closer it came; once more the whip cracked and the post horn blared, and now the promised extra coach rolled into the light of the station lantern. And before the horses had been brought to a halt, Carsten saw the form of a tall man nimbly jump from the coach and walk towards him. "Heinrich!" he called and rushed forwards, so that he almost stumbled, but the man turned to the girl, who now flung her arms around him with a cry of joy. "I began to think you weren't going to come any more!"

"I? Not come? On Christmas Eve? Oh!"

Carsten watched as the two went down the street arm in arm through the falling snow; when he turned around, even the place before the station, where the coach had halted, was empty. "He did not come, he probably was sick," he said to himself in a low voice.

Then a broad hand was laid on his arm. "Oho, my friend," spoke Mr Jaspers's familiar voice close by, "didn't I know you'd be in low spirits? Sick, you say? No, Carsten, don't let that worry spoil your Christmas Eve. Why, you know, in Hamburg there are all kinds of ways for young fellows to spend Christmas besides being in your old great-grandfather's house on the alley. But see here, wasn't it nice of me to help you wait? Now you'll have company on the way back!"

Mr Jaspers's voice had taken on an almost tender expression, but Carsten did not heed it. On the way home, too, he let Mr Jaspers trot at his side undisturbed; he had become a patient man.

When he stepped into his house again, he heard the room door being quickly closed from the inside. "Just one moment's patience!" Anna's clear voice called; then the door was opened wide, and the slender girlish form stood on the threshold as in a frame. Nor did she step out, she stared without stirring at her old foster father.

"Alone, Uncle?" she finally asked.

"Alone, my child."

Then the two of them went in to join Aunt Brigitta in the festively decorated room, and while Carsten silently sat by in the leather armchair, the two women exhausted the possibilities in searching for new suppositions as to what it might have been that had ruined their holiday happiness, until finally the evening had passed, and they silently put out the lights and removed the gifts which they had arranged so zealously just a short while before.

The Christmas holidays had passed too without Heinrich's appearing or any message from him having been received. When New Year's Eve too arrived, and the long awaited hour of mail delivery again passed by, the worries of these previous days had increased in the old man to the point of almost suffocating fear. What could have happened? What if Heinrich lay sick there in the big strange city? The deliberations of the women, calmer this time, were not able to restrain him; he had to go and see for himself. In vain they pictured to him the hardships of the long journey in the bitter cold that had set in; he gathered together the necessary money for the trip and asked Brigitta to pack his bag; then he went into town to see about a conveyance for the next morning.

When he arrived at home, completely exhausted after much running around, he found that a letter had come from Heinrich; an error of the postman had delayed it. Hurriedly he broke the seal; his hands shook so that he could hardly get the spectacles out of his pocket. But it was quite a cheerful letter; Mr Jaspers had been right; nothing special had happened to Heinrich, he had only thought it was better to enjoy the Christmas Fair in Hamburg and then come home later, when the big pear tree in the yard would be in bloom, and when they could walk out on the dike together. A jolly description of various parties and programs followed; he seemed to have had no suspicion of the anxieties he had caused his family.

The letter also contained a postscript: he and a good friend had started out for themselves on some business deals that had already earned them a nice profit; he knew now where money was to be got, and they would soon have quite different news from him. Of course he had not mentioned how risky, in more than one respect, this business connection was for him.

Carsten, having read everything and then reread it, leant back wearily in his chair; the name "Juliana" involuntarily pushed out through his lips. But at any rate Heinrich was well; nothing bad had happened.

"Well, Uncle?" asked Anna, who stood before him with Aunt Brigitta, waiting for the news.

He handed them the letter. "Read it yourselves," he said, "perhaps I'll be able to sleep better tonight. And then, Anna, tell the driver he need not bring the carriage, my old legs can't make it any more."

He looked almost happy at these words; a resting place had arrived, and he would try to make thorough use of it.

The next morning the Christmas gifts were taken out of the drawers again, carefully packed into a small box, and mailed to Heinrich; on top lay a letter from Anna, full of sincere admonitions and full of honest indignation. After a few months she received as reply a candy Easter egg which could be opened, and out of which a gold brooch emerged; some bantering jingles, thanking her for her good advice, were wound about it on a strip of paper.

If the gold brooch was a yield of the business deals he had contrived, it certainly remained the only sign of them that reached home; in the scanty letters these were either not mentioned at all or only in general intimations.

Time moved along after the Easter holidays, and now the afternoon of Pentecost had arrived. The two women were in the sunny vestibule, busily working; Aunt Brigitta had the curtain moulding of the shop window lying before her on the counter, endeavouring to pin a fresh white curtain on it; Anna, with a number of green woodruff wreaths hanging over one arm, was reaching for nails or hooks on the freshly kalsomined wall opposite, on which to hang the festive decorations. Two of the wreaths were nicely placed, but the nail for the third one was too high, so that the slender girl's outstretched arm could not reach it with the wreath.

"Child, child!" cried Aunt Brigitta from the counter, "you're boiling hot; why don't you fetch a stool?"

"No, Auntie, it must be possible!" replied Anna laughing, and with zestful groans she began to renew her useless exertions.

Suddenly the front door was thrown open, so that the ringing of the bell sounded deafeningly through the hall; amid the ringing a youthful man's voice cried, "A man's hand up there!" and in one and the same moment the wreath was removed from Anna's outstretched hand and hung on the nail. Anna found herself in the arms of a handsome man with tanned face and impressive sideburns, whose dress was unmistakably that of a city dweller. But she had already pushed him from her with such a vigorous thrust that he flew straight towards Aunt Brigitta, who threw up her hands in front of her moulding. At this the poor victim burst into a merry laugh which drowned out the dying tones of the doorbell.

"Heinrich, Heinrich, it's you!" cried the women in unison.

"This is what they call a surprise, Aunt Brigitta, isn't it?"

"Boy," said the old lady, still somewhat vexed, "in your stylish coat there's still the same old blow-hard; when you announce your coming, we can wait till we die, and when you come you could frighten us to death."

"Oh well, Aunt Brigitta, you'll be rid of me again soon enough; a fellow like me hasn't much time for loafing."

"Oh, Heinrich," said the good aunt, eyeing him with evident satisfaction, "it wasn't meant like that! How well you're looking, boy. But now help me a minute too with your nice tall body."

With one jump Heinrich was over the counter and immediately thereafter he was standing on the window seat, holding in his hands the moulding with the white curtains hanging from it.

A short time later, when the arrival of the master of the house was announced by the measured ringing of the doorbell, Heinrich was already sitting, with his wants attended to, in the good room at the coffee table, proclaiming to the eager listeners the wonders of the big city and his own activities. Immediately thereafter he stood face to face with his father, who grasped both his hands and with bated breath looked into his eyes. "My son!" he said finally, and Heinrich felt how a quiver passed from the old man's body into his own.

For a long time, even after they were sitting with the others at table, the father's gaze remained fixed on the face of his son, whose quickly restored flow of speech passed his ears without being really understood. Heinrich seemed to him to be outwardly almost a stranger; the resemblance to Juliana had lessened, he told himself with painful satisfaction; the time of his departure from his native town, even though only a few years had passed since then, now lay far behind him. A happy thought suddenly filled the father's heart; whatever had happened at that time, it had been only the fault of a boyish young man still in the process of development, the responsibility for which could no longer be loaded upon the man now sitting before him. Carsten involuntarily folded his hands; when Anna's eyes happened to turn towards him, she too stopped listening to Heinrich's wonderful tales: her old uncle sat there as if he were praying.

Later, to be sure, when son and father were sitting alone face to face, Heinrich had to give an account of himself to his father, too. He was now on a business trip for his firm, he said; he would have to leave the very next day, travelling northward. From the elegant notebook which Heinrich took out of his pocket, Carsten was initiated into various details, and he nodded contentedly, seeing his son in well-organized work. Less intelligible were the bits of information given out by Heinrich about his independent business deals; he managed to pass these over with casual intimations, while he explained in great detail the new enterprises which were to be launched with the indubitable profits of the first ones. Carsten had no experience in such matters, but when the projects went higher and higher in Heinrich's voluble exposition, and the money flowed in from richer and richer sources, then at times he felt as if Juliana's features were looking at him from his son's face, and in fear as well as affection he grasped his son's hands, as if by so doing he could keep him on solid ground.

However, when they sat together in church the next forenoon, he could not deny himself a slight satisfaction as on all benches heads were turned above hymnals towards the fine-looking young man; indeed, he was almost sorry that today Mr Jaspers was not also singing hymns at them from his customary pew.

In the afternoon, while Carsten and Brigitta were taking their naps in the house, Heinrich and Anna sat outside on the bench under the pear tree. They too were enjoying their afternoon rest, only their young eyes did not close like the old ones inside; they did not speak, to be sure, they listened to the summer song of the bees, coming down to them from the tree, its white blossoms covering it like snow. At times, and then more and more often, Anna would turn her head and secretly study the face of her childhood playmate, who was writing in the sand with his cane the name of a celebrated equestrienne. She still could not figure it out: the bearded man at her side, whose voice had an entirely different sound, was he still the Heinrich of yore? Just then a starling flew down from the roof onto the curb of the well, looked at her with its bright eyes, and began to chatter with puffed out throat, as if it wished to recall to her memory who had once sat there in its place. Anna opened her eyes wide and gazed up at a speck of blue sky visible through the branches of the tree; she feared the shadow which threatened to fall upon this golden summer day from the corner by the well.

But Heinrich's memory had likewise been awakened by the garrulous bird; only his eyes saw no shadows whatever coming from any corner. "What do you think, Anna," he said, pointing to the well with his cane, "do you believe I really would have jumped into that stupid well, that day?"

She was almost startled by these words. "If I had to believe it," she replied, "then you certainly would not have been worth my pulling you back from it."

Heinrich laughed. "You women are poor at figuring. Then you could certainly have let me sit there."

"Oh, Heinrich, say rather that nothing like that can ever, ever happen again!"

Instead of answering he took his costly gold watch from his pocket and let it dangle on its chain before her eyes. "We're making our own business deals now," he said then. "Only a few more months, then I'll throw those few paltry talers at the feet of the Senator's heirs; if they don't want to pick them up, they can let them lie; for of course a thing like that must be paid."

"They'll accept it all right, if you offer it to them modestly."

"Modestly?" He had placed himself before her and was looking into her face, which she had lifted up to him from her sitting position. "Well, if you think that," he added somewhat absently, while his eyes assumed the expression of attentive observation. "Do you know, Anna," he suddenly cried, "that you really are a deucedly pretty girl?"

The words had the ring of such spontaneous admiration that Anna became almost embarrassed. "I think you've brought home other eyes from Hamburg," she said.

"Right, Anna; I can see more now! But do you realize that you'll soon be twenty-three years old? Why don't you have a husband yet?"

"Because I didn't want one. What questions you ask, Heinrich!"

"I know very well what I'm asking, Anna; marry me, then you'll be rid of all embarrassment."

She looked at him in anger. "That is not a nice joke."

"And why should it be a joke?" he replied, trying to seize her hand.

She stood up, almost as tall as he. "Never, Heinrich, never." And when she had ejaculated these words, shaking her head vehemently, she freed herself and went back into the house, but she had flushed up to the blonde hair on her brow.

The business transactions from which Heinrich had promised himself mountains of gold must have had a different outcome after all. In less than a month after his departure, letters arrived from Hamburg, some from Heinrich himself and others from third parties, the contents of which Carsten managed to conceal from the women, yet which caused him to request a confidential interview with his old friend the mayor, who was well versed in civil as well as criminal law. And the very next evening in the city *Ratskeller* Mr Jaspers was already whispering over his wineglass to his neighbour, the city inspector of weights and measures: old Carstens, the fool with the dissolute son, was reliably reported to have cashed several of his best mortgage loans that very forenoon at a substantial discount. The other knew even more: the money, a large sum, had been mailed to Hamburg that same afternoon. They agreed that something must have happened there which demanded immediate and imperative help. "Help!" repeated Mr Jaspers, with his thin lips sipping smugly the last drops of his red wine. "Hans Christian wanted to help the rat, too, and poured boiling water into the rat trap."

At any rate, if there had really been danger, it seemed for the present to have been averted; even Mr Jaspers could not ferret out anything further, and whatever had buzzed around in town gossip gradually died out. Only in Carsten himself a striking change was noticeable from this time on; his commanding figure seemed suddenly to have shrivelled, the quiet assurance of his bearing appeared to have been blotted out, and while at one time he evidently sought to evade people's glances, at another time he seemed almost anxiously to seek in them an approval which he had otherwise found only in himself. He could become violently startled at all sorts of insignificant things; for instance, if there was an unexpected knock on his door, or if the postman entered in the evening, without his having seen him from the window. One might have thought that in his old age Carsten had acquired a bad conscience.

The women saw this, and they probably had their own ideas; for the rest, however, Carsten bore his burden alone; only at times he expressed his regret that he had not devoted his whole energy to the enlargement of the business he had inherited, so that Heinrich could now take it over and live near them all. Matters were not at their best in the house on the alley; for Aunt Brigitta too, whose worried looks were always following her brother, was ailing; only from Anna's eyes shone ever and again the unconquerable cheerfulness of youth.

It was on a hot September afternoon that the doorbell rang and Aunt Brigitta, who had been busy in the kitchen with Anna, stepped into the vestibule. "In Heaven's name," she cried, "here comes the bearer of bad news, as the mayor calls him. What does he want of us?"

"Away with bad luck," said Anna, pounding the underside of the table with the knife in her hand. "Shouldn't that help, Auntie?"

By now the disparaged one was standing before the open kitchen door. "Ah, the best of good days to all of you!" he called out with his old-womanish voice, mopping away the drops of perspiration from the hairy fringes of his fox-red wig with his blue-checked handkerchief. "Well, how are you, how are you? Is friend Carsten at home? Always busily at work?"

But before he could receive an answer, he had curiously scrutinized the old spinster. "Well, well, Briggy, you look bad; you've lost ground since we last saw each other."

Aunt Brigitta nodded. "You're right, I don't feel too well, but the doctor thinks I'll improve now in this nice weather."

Mr Jaspers emitted a chuckle. "Yes, yes, Briggy, that's what the doctor thought about little Danish Marie in the convent, when she had consumption. You know she always called her little room 'my tiny paradise'," again he chuckled in amusement, "but still she had to leave her tiny paradise."

"God protect us in his grace," cried Aunt Brigitta, "you old person, your talk's enough to bring death on our heels."

"Now, now, Briggy, old spinsters and ashen stakes keep for many a year!"

"But now you hurry and get out of my kitchen, Mr Jaspers," said Brigitta. "My brother can deal better with your compliments."

Mr Jaspers retired; at the same time, however, he lifted the steaming wig from his bald pate and held it out to Anna on one finger. "Young lady," he said, "be kind enough to hang this thing up awhile on your picket fence, but be a little careful that the cat doesn't get it."

Anna laughed. "No, no, Mr Jaspers; you just carry out your old monstrosity yourself. And our cat, she doesn't eat such red rats."

"Is that so! You're really a saucy thing," said the bearer of bad news, inspected briefly his detached hair adornment, dried it with his blue-checked handkerchief, clapped it on his head again, and at once disappeared in the doorway of the living room.

When Carsten, who had been sitting over his account books, saw the eyes of Mr Jaspers, glittering with officiousness, appear in the doorway, he laid down his pen with a hasty motion. "Well, Jaspers," he said, "what news are you taking out for a walk today?"

"True enough, true enough, my young friend," replied Mr Jaspers, "but you know – one man's meat is another man's poison!"

"Well, then make it brief and empty out your pockets!"

Mr Jaspers seemed not to notice the tense look from the wide-open, deep-set eyes directed to his wrinkled little face. "Patience, patience, friend," he said, smugly drawing a chair close to him, "it's this way: the little shopkeeper in South Street, where the people of Ostenfeld get their necessities, you know him, I'm sure; the little fellow always had a shiny, well-combed tuft of hair on his head, but that didn't help him either, Carsten, not a farthing's worth. I hope you aren't related in any way to this little pewit."

"You mean on my money's side? No, no, Jaspers, but what about him? It was a good living while his parents had it."

"Indeed it was, Carsten, but a good living and a stupid fellow, they never stay together long; he has to sell. I have it in my hands; four thousand talers down, five thousand registered debts included in the deal. Well? Now you stare at me? But I thought at once, that would be something for your Heinrich that doesn't come your way every day."

Carsten heard this but didn't dare to answer; he rummaged nervously among the papers on his desk. But then he said, and his words seemed to be spoken with difficulty. "That won't work out yet; my Heinrich must first age some more."

"Age some more?" Mr Jaspers laughed again with great amusement. "That's what our pastor thought about his boy too, but what was born a donkey, friend, will never become a horse."

Carsten felt a strong urge to show his guest the door, but he feared instinctively that that would be throwing this chance through the door too.

"No, no, friend," the other went on calmly, "I have better advice. You must find him a wife: understand me, a capable one, and one who also has a few thousand in credit. Well," and with his red wig he made a motion towards the kitchen "you have everything close by."

Carsten said almost mechanically, "How you worry about other people's children!"

But Mr Jaspers had stood up and slyly looked down at the sitting man. "Think it over, friend, I still have to go to the finance board; I'll keep the deal open for you till tomorrow."

With these words he was already out of the door. Carsten remained seated at the table with his head propped up; he did not see that immediately thereafter, as Mr Jaspers's top hat was pushing past the windows outside, the importunate little eyes cast one more sharp glance into the room.

The suggestions of the "city's bearer of bad news" seemed nevertheless to have had an after-effect. That was just what Carsten had been trying to find for such a long time; the business offered for sale, to be sure now badly neglected, could under good management be considered a secure investment with a not too high rate of interest. Here in town the father could keep an eye on it himself, and in time Heinrich would learn to stand on his own feet. Carsten took heart; with trembling hand he once more took from his desk drawer those Hamburg letters that had not long ago cost him the greatest part of his small property: and he carefully read them through, one by one. Enclosed in the last one was a receipted note; the name under the acceptance had been crossed out to make it illegible.

How often he had looked through those letters to convince himself over and over again that everything was in order now, that no disaster could develop from them in the future. But now they should at last be destroyed. He tore them into shreds and threw them into the stove, where the first winter fire should soon wholly consume them.

He closed the door of the stove as softly as if he had secretly committed an evil deed. Then for a long time he stood before his open desk, the key in his hand; he was breathing with difficulty, and his grey head sank ever deeper on his chest. But still, and again and again this appeared before his eyes, the deeds to which his weak son had been misled by big city conditions, would be impossible here in the small town! If only he could have him here soon, right now! A feverish fear seized him that his son might just now, at the last moment, when the safe harbour was perhaps ready to receive him, be once more tempted into that whirlpool.

The desk was to be sure finally locked, but for about an hour the otherwise never idle man walked aimlessly back and forth in the house and yard, now speaking a few words to the women about matters which otherwise had never concerned him, now walking through the hall into the yard to inspect the well curb, long since repaired. Returning from there, he opened a door that led from the hall into an annex and to Juliana's death chamber in its upper storey. The narrow stairway, unused for years, creaked under his steps, as if the old time were awakening from its sleep. Up in the bedroom, below the window that faced the gloomy alley, stood an empty bedstead, half destroyed by worms. Carsten drew up the only chair and sat here long. Before his eyes the bare boards filled; from white pillows a pale countenance with two dying eyes gazed at him, as if now they would promise him what it was too late to grant.

Not until late that afternoon did Carsten again sit at his work table. But it was not the usual matters that he worked at today;

a trusteeship accounting, even though it was to be turned in at a bankruptcy hearing the next day, had been pushed aside and instead a little book taken out of his desk which contained the information about his own financial situation; his big dark eyes wandered restlessly across the open pages. The old man sighed: the best items were crossed out in red. Nevertheless he began carefully to figure out his status: what assets were still on hand and what he could expect in the future. As there was not enough, he calculated besides the value of his little marsh fen, which he had continued to hold up to now, but land values at that time were inconsequential. He thought of accepting, in addition to his other duties, another city position that had recently been offered him, but which he had not ventured to accept because of his weakened health; now he thought he had been too timid; he would apply for the post, still vacant, the very next day. And he started afresh to figure out his assets, but the hoped-for result refused to appear. He laid down his pen and wiped the perspiration from his grey hair.

Then Mr Jaspers's advice sounded in his ears, and his thoughts began to wander about in the well-to-do homes of the town. Yes indeed, there were girls to be found there, and a few of them, so he thought, probably firm enough to sustain a weak husband, but would he dare to knock on their doors for his Heinrich?

While he was answering this question himself with a slow shake of the head, Anna stepped into the room in all the cheerful resoluteness of her character; his eyes lit up, and involuntarily he reached out both arms to her.

Anna looked at him in surprise. "Did you want something, Uncle Carsten?" she asked, him in a friendly tone.

Carsten dropped his arms. "No, child," he said almost embarrassed, "I didn't want anything. Don't let me disturb you, I suppose you were going to get supper ready."

He took up his pen again, as if to continue with the calculations lying before him, but his eyes remained fixed on the girl, while she moved the folding table from the wall into the room and then, almost noiselessly, with her sure hand set the things on the table for their usual evening meal. A vision of the future arose in his soul, before which he laid down all his worries. But no, no; he had always faithfully cared for this child! Ah, if that last affair had not happened!

He got up and stepped before his simple family picture. As he gazed at it, the painted sunset seemed to glow, and the silhouettes began to take on bodies. He nodded to them; yes, indeed, that was his father, his grandmother; these were honest people who were strolling there. When the family soon afterwards was sitting together at supper, Brigitta's sisterly eyes searched deeper and deeper in her brother's face, which could not conceal a troubled expression. "Get rid of it, Carsten!" she finally said, grasping his hand. "What burden of disaster did that miserable man load off on you this time?"

"Not exactly a disaster, Brigitta," replied Carsten, "only a hope that cannot be fulfilled." And then he reported to the women the offer of the little business, his wishes, and finally, that it could not be done after all.

Silence followed these words. Anna looked at the tea leaves in her empty cup: but she found no oracle there, as old women claim to do. Her small fortune was again oppressing her; finally she summoned her courage and, raising her eyes to her foster father, she said softly, "Uncle!"

"What is it, child?"

"Don't be angry at me, Uncle. But you did not calculate well."

"Not calculate well? Anna, do you claim to do it better?"

"Yes, Uncle," she said firmly, and bright tears welled from her blue eyes, "aren't my stupid talers to be of any use this time either?"

Carsten looked over at her silently for a while. "I might have expected that of you," he said then, "but no, Anna, not this time either."

"Why not? Tell me, why not?"

"Because such an investment of your money offers no security."

"Security?" She had jumped up, and grasping both his hands she knelt before him; her young face, now raised up to him, was flooded with tears. "Oh, Uncle, you are old now; you can't stand this; you should not have so many worries!"

But Carsten pushed her from him. "Child, child, you want to lead me into temptation; neither I nor Heinrich may accept such an offer."

Appealing for help, Anna turned her head towards Aunt Brigitta; she however sat like a statue, her hands folded in front of her on the table. "Well, Uncle," she said, "if you refuse me, then I'll write to Heinrich myself."

Carsten gently laid his hand on her head. "Against my will, Anna? That you will not do."

The girl was silent a moment, then she lightly shook her head under his hand. "No, Uncle, that's true, not against your will. But don't be so hard; after all, his happiness is at stake."

Carsten raised up her face from his knees and said, "Yes, Anna, I am thinking that too, but only one may set the stake: the one who also gave him life. And now, my dear child, no more of this matter!" He gently pushed her from him; then he pushed back his chair and went out.

Anna's gaze followed him; soon however she jumped up and threw herself into Aunt Brigitta's arms.

"We'll leave it to God," said the old lady, "this time I understand my brother very well." Then she held the big child in her arms for a long while.

Carsten had gone into the yard. It was dark as he sat under the old family tree, which was long since bare of fruits and from whose crown he heard the leaves dropping to the ground one by one. He thought back to the past, and soon visions appeared and disappeared of themselves. The form of his beautiful wife passed by him, and he reached his arms into space; he himself did not know whether towards her or towards his distant son, who bound him still more indissolubly to her shade. Then again he saw himself sitting on the bench where he was now sitting, but as a boy, with a book in his hand; the voice of his father came to him from the house, and little Peter came riding his hobbyhorse into the yard. Soon however he had to ask himself why this peaceful scene now filled him with such pain. Then it suddenly came over him: "Then, yes, then he had lived his life himself; now another was doing that; he had nothing more that belonged to him alone – no thoughts – no sleep..."

He let his weary body sink against the tree trunk; the gentle falling of the leaves struck his ears almost soothingly.

But something more was to happen before this day came to an end. Inside, Brigitta had finally sat down in her accustomed manner before the spinning wheel, and Anna began to clear the table. As she stepped into the hall with the dishes, the mail carrier was just passing. "For the Mademoiselle," he said and handed her a letter through the half-opened front door. By the candle burning on the store counter Anna recognized with astonishment Heinrich's writing on the envelope; he had never before written to her like this. Deep in thought she took the candle, and as she entered the kitchen, she pulled the door shut.

It was a long time before she came into the living room again, but Brigitta had noticed nothing, her spinning wheel purred on evenly, while Anna now as on all days folded the table together and placed it against the wall again. Only it was done somewhat more noisily and uncertainly today; she mentioned the letter neither to the old lady nor to her foster father, when he came into the room after a while and sat down to his books.

Finally the women went upstairs to their joint bedroom, which faced the yard. The windows had stood open and let in the fresh evening air, but Anna could find no sleep; the wind carried the sound of the church clock at long measured intervals into the rustling of the pear tree, and she counted one hour after the other.

Nor did Brigitta find her rightful sleep today; for she sat up and looked towards the girl's bed that stood against the wall opposite her own. "Child, haven't you slept yet?" she asked.

"No, Aunt Brigitta."

"You're worrying about my old brother, aren't you? But I know him, don't ask him about it again; he would never have peace of mind again if you'd been able to persuade him."

Anna did not answer.

"Are you sleeping, child?" Brigitta asked again.

"I will try to sleep, Auntie."

Brigitta did not ask again; Anna soon heard her breathing in quiet slumber.

It was almost forenoon when the young girl awoke from a deep sleep, which had finally overtaken her and from which her good aunt had not wanted to wake her. She dressed quickly and went downstairs, where through the open door of the front room she saw Brigitta busy at one of the large cupboards; yet she did not go to her, but into the kitchen, where she sat down on the wooden chair near the stove. After she had poured herself a cup of the coffee that had been kept warm for her, sitting idly before it and then drinking half of it, she got up with a determined movement and at once stepped into the living room.

Carsten was standing at the window, idly gazing out at the harbour. Now he slowly turned to the entering girl. "You weren't able to sleep," he said, giving her his hand.

"Oh, but I was, Uncle; I made up for it."

"But you are pale, Anna. You are too young to lose sleep over others' worries."

"Others', Uncle?" She looked calmly into his eyes a while. Then she said, "I had much to think about for myself as well."

"Then tell me about it, if you think I can advise you."

"Just tell me," she hastily replied, "is that shop in South Street still to be had? I didn't sleep too long? Mr Jaspers hasn't been here again?"

Carsten said almost harshly, "What does this mean, Anna? You know that I shall not buy it."

"I know that, Uncle, but—"

"Well, Anna, what do you mean: but?"

She had stepped close to him. "You said yesterday that I might not furnish the stake for Heinrich's happiness, but – even if you were right yesterday, now overnight things have changed."

"Stop that, child!" said Carsten. "You will not persuade me."

"Uncle, Uncle," cried Anna, and a joyful tenderness rang from her voice, "there's no help for you now, for your Heinrich has asked me to be his wife, and I shall say yes."

Carsten stared at her as if struck by lightning. He sank down on the leather armchair beside him, and waving his arms as if he must push away invisible foes he cried out vehemently, "You want to sacrifice yourself! Because I would not take your money alone, now you give yourself into the bargain!"

But Anna shook her head. "You are mistaken, Uncle. Although you are all very dear to me, I could never do that; I am not that kind of person."

Timidly, as if his words could destroy the approaching happiness, Carsten replied, "How is this? You two were always only like brother and sister."

"Yes, Uncle," and an almost roguish smile passed over her pretty face. "I thought that too, but all at once it was no longer like that." Then suddenly growing serious, she pulled a letter from her pocket. "Here, read it yourself," she said, "I received it yesterday before going to bed."

His hands reached for it, but they were trembling so that his eyes could hardly take in the lines.

What she had given him was the letter of a homesick man. "I'm no good here," wrote Heinrich, "I must go home, and if you'll stay with me, you, Anna, for my whole life, then I'll be good, then everything will turn out well."

The letter had fallen on the table; Carsten had drawn the girl down to him with both arms. "My child, my dear child," he whispered to her, while tears welled incessantly from his eyes, "yes, stay with him, do not leave him; he was such a good little boy."

But suddenly, as if driven by an inner fear, he forced her away from him again. "Have you thought it over, Anna?" he said. "I could not advise you to become my son's wife."

A slight tremor sped across the girl's face, while the old man sat before her with tight lips. She nodded to him several times: "Yes, Uncle," she said then, "I know that he is not the most responsible person, otherwise you would not have such worries, but what happened here that time, years ago, you once said yourself, Uncle, it was partly a boy's prank, and even if he has not yet made up for it, still nothing like that has ever occurred again."

Carsten made no reply. His glance went involuntarily towards the stove, in which the scraps of those letters were lying. If he were to get them out now! If he were to fit them together piece by piece before her eyes! Neither Anna nor Brigitta knew of these affairs.

His tears had dried, but he took out his handkerchief to wipe beads of perspiration from his brow. He tried to speak, but the words would not pass his lips.

The lovely blonde girl again stood erect before him; with growing fear she tried to read the thoughts from his silent countenance.

"Uncle, Uncle!" she cried. "What has happened? You've been so quiet and worried recently." But as he looked up at her beseechingly, she stroked his furrowed cheek with her hand. "No, don't worry so much; accept me with confidence as your daughter; you shall see what a good wife can do."

And as he now looked into her courageous young eyes, he was no longer able to utter the words which could destroy his child's happiness at one stroke.

Suddenly Anna, who had just looked out of the window, grasped his hands. "There's Mr Jaspers!" she said. "Now you'll arrange everything between you, won't you?" And without waiting for an answer she quickly went out the door.

Now his tongue was released. "Anna, Anna!" he called; like a cry for help the name rushed from his mouth. But she did not hear it any more; instead, Mr Jaspers's fox-red wig showed itself through the door to the living room, and with him visions of a flattering future forced themselves into the room, and, unconcerned about the darkness behind them, helped to close the deal.

Kramer Street begins with the corner house of the alley, running east from the harbour, and the row of houses opposite, past the market place, continues as South Street. There in a roomy house lived Heinrich and Anna. On market days the spacious hall of the house, in front of the store, again teemed with shopping farmers, and Anna had more than enough to do to urge the more important ones into the good room for refreshments and conversation; for the easy and sociable manner of her husband had not only brought back customers but increased their number.

Carsten could not refrain from looking in on his children every day. He could be seen walking at a definite hour of each and every forenoon along the charming path that led behind the backyards of those streets from the harbour, where the sluice makes a break towards the east in the row of houses. But he took his time; leaning on his faithful cane he would often stand in the shade of the high hedges and look across to the meadows through which the tide flow pushes out into the green land; held back now by the sluice, to be sure, yet in autumn or winter perhaps rushing over it, flooding the meadows and ruining the gardens. Such reflections set the old man's cane and legs in motion again: he must warn Anna at once that in October she should take her fine celery from the ground betimes. When he had reached the lattice gate to Anna's garden, the tall womanly figure usually approached him on the long sidewalk; indeed, when summer came around for the second time, she did not come alone; she carried a boy in her arms, who was her very own and had been christened after his father. And how becoming the maternal conduct was, when, laying her shining cheek against that of her child, she would walk down the garden, singing softly. Even Carsten now had company on these walks; for Brigitta too, in spite of her advanced decrepitude, had been set in motion by the child. Hardly had the young woman stepped out from among the trees with her child when the aged siblings at the gate were calling to them affectionately. Brigitta would nod and Carsten would wave his cane in greeting, and when they finally had come close, Brigitta could hardly get her fill of looking at the child, still less Carsten of eyeing its mother.

This happiness passed, and indeed it was already gone while Carsten and Brigitta still believed themselves to be basking in its light; their eyes were no longer sharp enough to notice the fine lines that were beginning to engrave themselves gradually between the mouth and cheeks of Anna's clear countenance.

Heinrich, who had at first taken hold of the business with his fiery zeal, so prone to fade rapidly, soon tired of the retail trade and the personal contact with country people which this entailed. An added misfortune at that time was the arrival of a boastful speculator only slightly older than Heinrich and related to him on his mother's side; he had been in England most recently and had brought back from there very little money, to be sure, but a head filled with half-ripe plans, for which he soon managed to kindle Heinrich's lively interest.

At first they tried to launch a cattle export trade to England, which up to then had been in the hands of a favourably situated neighbouring town. After this had failed, they had an oyster tank constructed below the dike, planning to have English native oysters outdo those of the local leaseholders; this undertaking however, hopeless in itself, also lacked the hand of an expert, and Carsten, whose previous warning had been disdained, had to cover one debt after another and take up one mortgage after another on his properties.

Anna now rarely saw her husband at home in the evening, for the unmarried cousin took him to a tavern where he liked to wind up the day's work. Here, over hot drinks, the transactions were discussed with which they would soon amaze the little town; later, when the head could no longer serve for this, cards were laid on the table, with which stakes and results showed up faster.

Yet for all that Heinrich had not lost interest in his wife. If fortune flung a momentary profit in his direction, which according to his way of thinking always made a rich man of him, he might spend half of it for gold chains or rings or costly stuffs to adorn her lovely body. But what was Anna, the wife of a small shopkeeper, to do with these things, especially since the entire running of the business gradually came to rest on her shoulders?

One Sunday – the first cargo of oysters had just been quickly and profitably sold – while Anna was walking the floor with her boy on her arm, Heinrich quickly and cheerfully entered the room. After he had rested his eyes on her face for awhile, he led her to the mirror and suddenly placed a necklace of individually set sapphires about her neck; happy as a child he gazed at her. "Well, Anna? Let these do until I can bring you diamonds!"

The boy reached for the glittering jewels and emitted sounds of delight, but Anna looked at her husband with alarm. "Oh, Heinrich, you love me, but you waste money! Think of yourself, of our child!"

At that the happiness in his face was extinguished; he took the jewellery from her neck and put it back into the case from which he had removed it. "Anna," he said after a while and almost humbly grasped his wife's hand, "I never knew my mother, but I have heard about her – not at home, for my father never spoke to me of her; an old captain in Hamburg, who was once her dancing partner in his youth, told me about her. She was beautiful, but she didn't care to be anything but beautiful and gay; perhaps her death was fortunate for my father. I often yearned for my mother, but her son, Anna – I think you would have done better not to take him as husband."

In passionate emotion the young wife flung her free arm about her husband's neck. "I know I am different from you, Heinrich, and from your mother, but for that very reason I am yours and am near you; please will to be near me too; don't always go away evenings, stop doing it for your old father's sake as well. He is worried when he knows you are in that company."

But the last words had already changed Heinrich's mood. He freed Anna's arm from his neck, and with a jest that passed over his lips somewhat unsteadily he said, "How can I help it if the wine I drink gives my father a headache?"

With a vehement movement Anna clasped the boy to her breast. "Be assured, Heinrich, I will faithfully see to it that this child will not some day say that of his father!"

"Oh come, Anna! I didn't mean anything bad when I said that."

No matter how it had been meant, it changed nothing, either. When during that time the night watchman approached Heinrich's house on his rounds, he often saw the young wife's head at the open window as she listened to the street in the quiet night; he knew her well, for he was the father of that neighbour's child which Anna had once so fondly dragged around. Respectfully, without being seen by her, he lifted his hat in passing, and not until he was far from her house did he call out the late hour. But Anna had counted each stroke of the clock, and when finally the familiar step could be heard coming up the street, it was usually not as steady as when she used to hear it during the day. Then she fled back into the room and threw her arms anxiously over her child's cradle.

The wise as well as the stupid townspeople had been shaking their heads for a long time, and evenings in the *Ratskeller* the fox-red wig on Mr Jaspers's head could be seen bobbing up and down as he laughed in glee; indeed he could not refrain from repeatedly telling his friend, the city inspector of weights and measures, that the house in South Street would soon pass once more through his dirty broker's hand.

In the meantime Carsten was waging a quiet, oft recurring battle with his own child. At the time of the marriage he had made the couple agree that a part of Anna's fortune should remain under his jurisdiction as her private estate; now this too was to be drawn into the partnership, but since Anna had become a mother, she considered this sum to be the property of her child and had placed everything in the faithful hands of her uncle and father. When his son had left him in anger after such discussions, the old man would look groaning towards the stove in which years before the remains of those letters were burnt, or he would stand before the family picture and carry on a silent, painful dialogue with the shadow of his own youth.

A seemingly insignificant circumstance added its weight. Old Brigitta suddenly fell sick one night – it might have been close to two o'clock in the morning – and since their domestic help was only there by day, Carsten himself set out to get the doctor.

On the way home he passed the before-mentioned tavern, whose windows were the only ones in the dark row of houses that sent lamplight into the street. There seemed to be no guests inside any more, for it was completely quiet. Carsten already had the house behind him when from it a hoarse sound came to his ears which caused him to stop suddenly; in this ugly human voice, in which another familiar one seemed to be hidden, there was something that frightened him almost to death. He could not walk on, he had to go back; prowling, eager to hear it again and this time more clearly, he stood under the window of the ill-reputed tavern. And again it came, wearily, as if emitted by a babbling tongue. Then the old man clasped his hands over his head and his cane fell with a clatter on the stone pavement.

Brigitta recovered slowly, as much as one can recover at seventy-five, but after that night Carsten had permanently lost his sleep. He always seemed to hear the hoarse voice of his son coming from that tavern, though it was several blocks away; he would sit up among his pillows and listen to the stillness of the night, but again and again at brief intervals that awful sound would be set free; his bony hand would reach into the darkness as if to grasp that of his son, but soon it would fall down limply over the edge of the bed.

His thoughts sped back to Heinrich's childhood; he tried to recall the happy face of the boy when he was told: "A walk along the dike"; he tried to hear his joyful cry when a lark's nest had been found or a large sea spider was drifted to the shore by the tide. Yet here too something came to share his poor sleep with him. Not only when the wind blew against his window from the sand flats, but even in nights as still as death, the monotonous roar of the sea was in his ears, now as always; it seemed to come as at ebb-tide from far out beyond the narrow channel; instead of the happy face of his child he saw the bare stretches of foaming mud flats shining in the moonlight, and out of them, flat and black, rose a desolate marsh islet. It was the one to which he had once rowed with Heinrich to look for gull or pewit eggs. But they had found none; only the stranded corpse of a drowned man. He lay among the primeval plants of the marsh grass, with large birds flying about him, his arms outstretched, his terrible dead countenance turned towards the sky. Screaming, with horrified eyes, the boy had clung to his father at this sight.

The old man tried again and again, even in his dreams, into which these imagined pictures followed him, to direct his thoughts towards more peaceful places, but each light breeze led him back to that terrible islet.

The days had changed, too; old Curator Carsten was still known under that name, to be sure, but he bore it almost as a retired official does his title, yet without any pension. Most of his former business transactions had passed into younger hands; only the small city job, which he really had procured that time, was still his, and the woollen goods business was also moving along under Brigitta's ageing hand, but more and more slowly.

It was an afternoon in the beginning of November. The wind blew steadily from the west; the arm with which the North Sea reaches into the city, in the shape of a narrow harbour, was filled with muddy-grey water which, boiling and foaming, had already flooded the landing steps in the harbour and was flinging the small island boats anchored there to and fro. Here and there people were already beginning to place before doors and basement windows the wooden bulwarks between whose double walls they would then pound down the manure which had been lying for weeks on all the adjacent streets.

Out of the house on the alley, escorted to the door by Brigitta, stepped a young sailor, who had equipped himself for the winter with a woollen jacket, but the storm ripped the paper from his package and the hat from his head.

"Oho, Miss Brigitta," he said as he raced after his hat, "the wind has changed; we'll have water today!"

"Oh Lord Jesus," screamed the old woman, "they're already putting up shutters everywhere! Christine, Christine!" and she turned towards a neighbour's child she was caring for while its parents were away. "The shutters must be brought up from the basement. Run to Kramer Street – Long Christian must come over at once!"

The child ran, but the storm seized it and would have thrown it against the houses like a poor bird, if Long Christian had not fortunately been coming already and brought the child back with him.

The bulwarks were fetched and set in front of the door up to half the height of a man. When twilight fell almost the whole square by the harbour was flooded; inhabitants of the houses near the ramparts were taken to higher parts of the city in boats. The sailboats below tore at their anchor chains, the masts pounded against each other; large white birds were hurled among them or clung shrieking to the fluttering tackle.

Brigitta and the child had watched Long Christian at work for a while; now they were sitting in the dark in the good room, behind securely screwed-on window shutters. Outside, the slapping of the water, the whistling in the ships' tackle, the shouting and the screaming of people, and how fiercely the gale tugged at the shutters as if it would tear them loose.

"Ohhh," said the child, "it's coming in, it's going to take me!"

"Child, child," said the old woman, "what are you talking about? What's coming in?"

"I don't know, auntie; what's outside there!"

Brigitta took the child on her lap.

"That is our dear God, Chrissy; what he does is well done. But come, let's go up to my room!"

During this time Carsten was occupied in the back hall; he was unpacking the old papers and ledgers stored in a cupboard and carrying them up to the bedroom in the annex; for in about an hour the tide would be high; today the lower floor was not safe from flooding.

He was just stepping back into the hall, a lit tallow candle in his hand; for lack of a table he placed the candle on the window seat, where the draft caused it to smoke, making the room with its massive cupboards seem all the gloomier; the storm, striking obliquely from the west, caused the leaden-framed window panes to rattle, as if at any moment they would be hurled down on the tile floor.

Regardless of this and in spite of the cries and shouts that reached him from the street, the old man seemed to be in no great hurry with his work. His house, made of stone, would surely remain standing; a different fall of his house stood before his soul, which he did not know how to prevent. That forenoon Anna had called on him, and, as the final salvation for her husband, had herself demanded of him the release of her bonds, but even to her, who had a right to make this demand, he had refused it. "Sue me; then they can be taken from me by the courts!"

Now he repeated to himself these words, with which he had dismissed her, and Anna's grief-distorted countenance arose before him, a silent accusation which he could not escape.

When he finally bent down at the cupboard again, he heard the outside door which led from the alley into the yard torn open by force, and soon the door from the yard to the hall was unlatched, and, as if hurled in by the storm, there stood in the middle of the dusky room a form which Carsten gradually recognized as that of his son.

But Heinrich did not speak, nor make any effort to close the door through which the storm was blowing in. Only after his father had asked him to, did he close it; yet as he did so the latch slipped out of his hand several times.

"You haven't wished me a good evening yet, Heinrich," said the old man.

"Good evening, father."

Carsten started when he heard this tone of voice; only once, only on one night had he heard it before. "What do you want?" he asked. "Why aren't you with your wife and child? The water must have reached your garden a long time ago."

What Heinrich answered was hardly to be heard above the roaring that surrounded the house.

"I don't understand you. What are you saying?" said the old man. "The money? Your wife's bonds? No, I will not give them up!"

"But – I'll be bankrupt – tomorrow!" The words had been convulsively uttered, and Carsten had understood them.

"Bankrupt!" As if stunned he repeated that one word. But now he stepped close to his son, and pressing his scrawny hand as in self-support against his chest, he said almost calmly, "I've gone far with you, Heinrich; may God and your poor wife forgive me for that. I will not go further; whatever comes tomorrow, we'll both atone then for our own guilt!"

"Father, my father!" stammered Heinrich. He seemed not to grasp the words that had been spoken to him.

In a sudden rush of emotion the old man stretched out both arms towards his son, and if the duskiness dominating the large room had permitted, and if Heinrich's eyes had been clear enough, he would surely have been frightened at the expression on his father's face, but the weakness which had overcome the latter for a moment passed.

"Your father?" he said, and his words sounded hard. "Yes, Heinrich! But I was also something else – people named me after it – only a piece of it have I still retained; see if you can tear it out of my old hands! For your wife shall not go begging, because her curator betrayed her for the sake of his wicked son!"

From outside a cry penetrated to them, and from distant streets came the muffled, traditional cry of distress: "Water, water!"

"Don't you hear?" cried the old man. "The sluice has given way. Why are you standing here? I have no more help for you."

But Heinrich did not answer, nor did he leave; with arms hanging limply he remained standing there.

Then, as on a sudden impulse, Carsten reached for the flickering candle and held it close before his son's face. Two dull, glassy eyes stared at him.

The old man staggered backwards. "Drunk!" he cried. "You are drunk!"

He turned away; holding the smoking candle before him with one hand, thrusting out the other hand defensively behind him, he swayed towards the door of the annex. As he stepped through it, he felt a tug at his coat, but he freed himself, and it grew dark in the hall, and from the other side the key was turned in the door lock.

The drunken man had suddenly regained his senses. As if awakening from the fog of a dream, he found himself alone in the familiar dark room; he suddenly knew every word that had been spoken to him. He groped along the locked door, he shook it. "Father, listen to me!" he called. "Help me, my father, only this one last time!" And again he shook the door, and once more he called with a loud voice. But whether the storm blew his voice away, or whether his father's ears were closed to him, the door was not opened; he heard nothing but the roaring in the air and in between the ravines of the yards and houses.

He stood there a while, his ear pressed against the door; then at last he left. But not through the yard towards the alley, where the door was perhaps still free of water; he went through the front hall to the bulwarks at the open door, halfway up which the water was already splashing. The moon had risen, but clouds were flying across the sky; light and darkness raced alternately over the foaming waters. Before him a mighty stream now seemed to be shooting down over the sluice, where through the gap between houses the way goes eastward towards the gardens and meadows; he thought he heard the death cry of the animals which the pitiless powers of nature were dragging past him there as in a frenzy. He shuddered. What was he doing here? But then at once he threw back his pallid, still youthfully handsome head.

"Oh, Jens!" he suddenly called; at one side among the houses he had caught sight of a boat, manned by two men, belonging to one of the former oyster ships. A defiant arrogance flashed from the eyes that a moment before had still been so dull. "Give me the boat, Jens! Or do you still have use for it?"

"Not this time," the answer rang back. "But where do you want to go, sir?"

"Where? Yes, where? There, just diagonally across to Kramer Street."

The little boat drew up to the bulwarks. "Get in, sir. But let us get out next door here at the butcher's."

Heinrich got in, and the two others were let out as they had requested. Yet as they stood there behind the bulwarks in the doorway, they soon saw that the boat was not steering into the safe path of the street, as Heinrich had declared. "Confound it," cried one of the men, "where are you going?"

Heinrich was still protected by the row of houses. "Home," he called back. "Home by the back way!"

"Sir, are you mad? That's not possible. The boat will overturn before you have rounded the sluice-way."

"It must be possible!" the voice came once more, partly blown away by the storm; then the boat shot out into the wild flood. For one moment more they saw it, like a shadow, thrown up and down by the waves; as it reached the gap between the houses above the sluice, it was seized by the current. The men uttered a cry: the boat had suddenly disappeared from view.

"It seemed to me," said Brigitta up in her room to the child, "as if I just now heard Uncle Heinrich's voice. But how should he get here?" Then she went out and called down into the dark hall from the stairway, "Heinrich, are you there, Heinrich?" Getting no answer, she shook her head and listened again, but only the water was splashing against the bulwarks.

She went all the way downstairs, with some difficulty, lit a candle, and placed it in the shop window; then, after she had inspected the height of the tide, she again went up to her room. "Be easy, Chrissy, the water won't come into the house today, but Uncle Heinrich wasn't here either."

Perhaps a quarter hour had passed; it seemed to have grown quieter outside, and people sat waiting in their houses. Then suddenly Brigitta put the child down from her lap. "What was that? Did you hear that,

Chrissy?" And again she ran to the stairs. "Is anyone down there?" she called down into the hall.

A man's voice answered through the open door.

"What do you want? Is it you, neighbour?" asked the old woman. "How did you get to our house?"

"I have a boat, Brigitta, but come down a moment."

As quickly as she could, with the child again clinging to her skirt, she went down the stairs. "What is it, neighbour? God protect us from misfortune!"

"Yes, Brigitta, yes, God protect us! But beyond Kramer Street on the fens there's a man in distress."

"Merciful God, a man! Do you want the big rope from our loft?"

The man shook his head. "It's too far, and the man is sitting on the tall barn post that is just barely above the water. Listen! You can hear him crying out. No, no, it was only the wind. But over there from the baker's attic they can see him."

"Stay here," said the old woman. "I'll call Carsten; maybe he'll know what to do."

They exchanged a few more words; then Brigitta ran to the back hall. But it was dark, Carsten was not there. When she and the child had groped their way to the corner of the annex, they found the door locked.

"Carsten, Carsten!" she called, beating against it with both hands. Finally steps came down the stairs, the key was turned, and Carsten stepped towards her, pale as death, holding the burnt-down candle in his hand.

"For Heaven's sake, brother, how you look! Why do you lock yourself in? What were you doing up there in the death chamber?"

He looked at her calmly, yet almost vacantly, wide-eyed. "What do you want, sister?" he asked. "Has the water started to fall?"

"No, brother, but there's been an accident." And she reported with rapid words what the neighbour had told her.

The stony form of the old man suddenly came to life. "A human being? A man, Brigitta?" he cried, seizing the arm of his old sister.

"Of course, of course; a man, brother!"

The child, who had not let go of Brigitta's skirt, now stuck out her little head. "Yes, Uncle Carsten," she said with an air of importance, "and the man is always calling for his father. From the baker's attic they can hear him yelling."

Carsten dropped the candle on the stone floor and rushed away. He was already down at the bulwarks and would have gone right into the water if the neighbour had not appeared in the nick of time and helped him into his boat.

A few moments later he was standing over on Kramer Street in the dark attic of the baker's house; through the open dormer window his gaze strayed out into the terror of the night.

"Where, where?" he asked, trembling.

"Just look straight ahead. The post on Peter Hansen's fen," answered the stout baker, who stood next to him, his thumbs in the armholes of his vest. "Only it's too dark now; you must wait until the moon appears again. But I'm going down; I am too soft-hearted; I can't bear to hear that yelling!"

"Yelling? I hear nothing!"

"You don't? Well, it can't help the one over there anyhow."

A blinding flash of moonlight broke through the racing clouds and lit up the ghastly pale face of the old man, who was holding his flying hair with both hands, while his wide-opened eyes anxiously roamed over the foaming water waste. Suddenly he gave a start.

"Carsten, what the devil, Carsten!" cried the baker, who in spite of his soft heart was still there; for at the same moment Carsten had fallen without a word into the arms of the portly man.

"Oh, that's it," he added, as he too took a look through the window. "The post – upon my soul – is empty! But what the deuce did that have to do with the old man?"

It was to be sure never determined who the man had been whose cry of distress had been drowned that night by the water, but it is certain that Heinrich did not return home either that night or later, nor was he ever seen again.

For the rest, Mr Jaspers's cheerful confidence was more than confirmed; not only the house in South Street but also the one on the alley soon went through his hands. Only Aunt Brigitta's coffin was still standing in the cool hall, from where it was carried out to its eternal rest. Carsten had to move out; while the auctioneer's gavel was ringing inside, he left his house leaning on Anna's arm, never to enter it again. Up on South Street, far beyond Heinrich's former business, where the last little houses are thatched with straw, there was now their joint home. Carsten no longer held any office, nor did he carry on any other business; for in that night he had had a stroke, and his mind had suffered; yet he was still quite capable of caring for little Heinrich, who had spent half the day on his grandfather's lap. The old man suffered no want, although Anna had also given up the last remnant of her assets for the sake of her husband's memory, but her hands and her courage never flagged. She had faded completely, having retained only her beautiful blonde hair; however, a spiritual beauty now shone from her countenance, which she had not possessed before, and whoever saw her in those days, the tall woman between the child and the man who had become a child, could not but remember the words of the Bible: though the body die, yet the soul will live.

It was a daily recurring joy to the old man, however, to seek and find the features of the mother in the little face of his grandson. "Your son, Anna; entirely your son!" he used to call out after long observation. "He has a happy face."

Then Anna would nod and say smiling, "Yes, grandfather, but the boy has your eyes!"

And so it goes on within the generations; hope grows with each human being, but no one thinks that with each morsel of food he also gives his child a piece of his own life, which soon can no longer be freed from his.

Blessed is he whose life is secure in the hand of his child, but also he for whom there remains, from all he once possessed, only a merciful hand to shake up the pillows for the last time under his poor head.

Notes

p. 30, *Schnaderhüpferl*: Short nonsensical folk songs (German dialect).

p. 67, *Nesi*: Storm names the child Nesi, familiar for Agnes; the woman's name is Ines in German. (TRANSLATOR'S NOTE)

p. 71, *Carsten Carstens*: Note that Storm distinguishes between "Carstens" as the public and "Carsten" as the family man. (TRANSLATOR'S NOTE)

p. 81, Lessing's *Nathan*: *Nathan the Wise* is a 1779 play by Gotthold Ephraim Lessing (1729–81), the German writer and critic.

p. 81, Hippel's *Careers in an Ascending Line*: A reference to the German writer Theodor Gottlieb von Hippel (1741–96) and his mostly autobiographical work *Lebensläufe nach aufsteigender Linie* (1778–81).

Printed in Great Britain
by Amazon